Uneasy bargain

"Half, Braden?" Gretchen smiled. "We'll split it up the middle."

"That's all?"

"And me," she amended. She walked to the window, pulled the cord to open the Venetian blind. Sunlight filtered through, dappled the room with light shadows. She unbuttoned the coat and tossed it on the chair. "I come with the deal."

She looked down at her body, then squared her shoulders until her upper half was stretched taut.

"What do I do with you?" Braden asked.

"That's easy." She walked toward him as though she were on a runway. "I'll be yours, Braden. Until you get tired of me. Then give me my cut and I'll get out of your way!"

Also by Jack Usher

REASON FOR MURDER
(Original title: *Brothers and Sisters Have I None*)

THE FIX

JACK USHER

WILDSIDE PRESS

The Fix

For Elmer M. Parsons

THE FIX

CHAPTER 1

IT WAS fifteen minutes until midnight. Under quiet Idaho skies, Nick Siroonian's Amalgamated Show was about to close for the night. The rest of the stores on Thieves' Alley were already rolled down and deserted. The talking people had left their positions in front of the strip joint, the Ten-in-one, and the noisy motordrome. The lights on the Ferris wheel were out, no longer circling their endless way through the dark night.

Stan Braden was working on a customer. He was going into the last hour of a successful night's play, hat shoved back on deep black hair, his eyes tired. He'd relieved a stubborn farmer of eighty-five dollars, then caught a young one for twenty more. Both men had walked away, neither believing it. Now a loner stood before his counter and was getting argumentative. Braden spoke.

"Look, mister, I'll count the marbles. You made a sixty-one. Sixty-two pays."

"Yes, but—"

"No buts. I'll draw it out for you. You dump the marbles on this board here. It's got holes with numbers. I count the holes with marbles in 'em. If you get a number that's posted on the board up there, you win. There! Is that so hard, friend?"

"I think I counted seventy-two," the red-faced townie said. "Anyways, you count too fast. You let me pick 'em up and you count—"

"How much you played, mister?" Braden stared bleakly at the man.

"Three dollars. You said—"

Braden took three one-dollar bills from his pocket and tossed them to the man. "There you are, Mac. Walk. Go

1

buy a candy cane." He reached for a rope, let tightly rolled canvas clatter between himself and the astonished red face. He began securing the booth for the night, muttering to himself.

He'd been away too long. He was still with it and for it, as the saying goes, but he didn't like this sort of life very much any more. After so many years away, he saw it with clearer vision, and maybe the romance had never really been there at all.

He scuffled through pine-scented wood chips and saw-dust, looked to where Crazy Joe was closing his food emporium. The odor of rancid grease and stale coffee drifted on the slight breeze. He walked on, only the lonely snarl of a departing wall-rider's motorcycle breaking the silence, past the idling generator truck to his place on the carnival lot. He unlocked the trailer door and entered, switching on the lights.

It was for sleeping and nothing else. To sleep in and to hold his personal belongings. He tossed his hat toward a bunk bed and looked around. Other than the bed, only a straight-backed chair could be classified as furniture. Four pieces of matched luggage were lined against one wall, and two small wardrobe trunks appropriated the space usually allotted to a trailer kitchen. A plastic bag, hanger protruding from the top, hung from the molding along one wall.

Braden walked to the bed and removed a bottle from under the pillow. He poured two inches of the whiskey into a water tumbler, then placed the bottle on top of one of the trunks. He moved to the plastic bag and unzipped it. He stared at the shoulder and one sleeve of the exposed black coat. As he drank, he ran the fingers of one hand over the slick, dark material.

It was proof of a sort—all that remained of the big ring, the big cars and the expensive women. He allowed the last swallow of liquor to pour down an open throat. The women he had enjoyed, he told himself. The other things? He shrugged. But the three-hundred-dollar Italian silk suit was proof—proof that he'd been a top bookie—a hustler who'd made it. Made it for a while, that is. He walked to the trunk and replenished his glass, then stooped and toasted himself sardonically in the mirror over the sink. He was too tall for the functional land cruiser. An inch over six feet, his one hundred and ninety pounds covered a well-muscled frame. Black hair, normally cut; grayish green eyes, ears set close to his head, thirty-four years of age. FBI records would show he had no visible scars or tattoos.

He wore expensive trousers and sports shirt, both in need of cleaning and pressing, and overly polished shoes. A carny, and dressed to prove it. It hadn't always been that way. He grimaced, looked in the mirror again. The day-old beard caused him to fill a container with water and place it on a small electric plate. When he finished his drink, he'd shave.

Braden flopped on the bunk, lay back and nursed the tumbler, staring blankly at the bare side of the trailer. Another lousy night, another one coming, and when in hell could he get out of this crum—

A knock sounded on the trailer door, and he scowled as he jumped up and closed the plastic bag, covering the suit.

"Come in!"

The door opened, and a girl stepped into the trailer. He recognized her. A redhead from the strip show. She lived alone in a trailer parked close to his.

"Busy, Stan?" She stood just inside the door, one hip pushed aggressively forward. Dressed in slacks and a pullover jersey, the tight sweater made her breasts blatant and distinct. Live bait.

"Just came in," he answered.

"You buying?" She was looking at the bottle.

"Help yourself."

While the girl found a glass and poured a drink, Braden studied her. Under twenty, he guessed. Still tightly fleshed and healthy. She wasn't pretty enough to work top strip palaces, but plenty good enough for the midway. Now. Until she began to sag and get lines in her face. She was the best he'd seen coming out of the flesh tent since he'd been back. The girl took her drink, fell back on the bunk, one leg swinging.

"We haven't seen you around the lot much, Stan."

"I haven't been around." He poured another shot in the glass, washed half of it around in his mouth and swallowed. He sat on the edge of the straight-backed chair.

The jersey and the top of the slacks had parted, and the girl idly scratched her bare stomach. She sipped some of the whiskey. "You gonna operate your store all season?"

"All season."

"You gonna stay alone?" Her hand had moved up and was working on ribs now, fingers lost under the cloth.

He shrugged, looked at the girl irritably. "Why in hell don't you take a shower and quit that God-damned scratching? On my bed!"

The girl moved her hand away quickly. She looked hurt.

"I showered right after the last show. It's this jersey. Makes me itch."

He didn't comment, drank some more.

"A couple of guys told me you had it made once. That right?" Her eyes measured him over the edge of her glass.

"Yeah, I had it made. For a long time I had it made." Braden stood, moved to the trunk and emptied the bottle into his glass. He was beginning to feel the liquor course through his veins, spreading in warming waves from his stomach.

"You went broke, huh?"

He laughed without mirth. "Broke? If that was all that happened, I'd be— Hey! What's your name?" He peered at the girl.

"Dolores, baby." She stretched, patting the side of the bunk. "Sit down, Stan."

"Just a minute." Braden opened a built-in cabinet and extracted a full bottle. He opened it, carried it to the bunk and sat by the girl. "You're alone, huh?"

"Yep. A few guys on the show have been shooting, but

I said no, and I'm gonna keep on saying no. Bunch of no-talents."

"Where's your old man, honey?"

He breathed the question, his hand trailing up her soft arm. The girl shivered. This wasn't the way, he knew. But the whiskey buzzed in him, and awareness of his long slide from success to second-rate carny hustling lay heavily on his spirit.

"No old man, baby. The guy that put me in the show got busted in Kansas. He's doing six months."

"For what?"

"Short-changing cashiers. They call it fraud by trick and device. The damned fool burned up a jerk town and finally ran into a guy that hollered." She took his hand and placed it on her stomach. "He won't be around all season."

Braden leaned forward and placed his lips over hers. Cheap perfume came from under the boat-necked jersey, clogging his nostrils. She pulled his hand from her stomach and moved it higher. When the kiss was over, he straightened.

"Hey," the girl said, making a long word of it. "I knew damned well I was holding off those crumbs for a reason. Do me some more, Stan."

"No." Braden stood unsteadily and looked down at her. "You'd better take a hike, kid."

The girl's small eyes widened. "What's the pitch? You too drunk or something?" She sat up. "I'll come back in—"

"Forget it." Braden moved to the chair. "Just forget it. No season, no playing house." He drank from his glass, then said to the girl, "Go find Eddie Bowers. He's going to run a wheel all year and he's looking for steady company."

She jumped to her feet. "I ain't good enough for you? Is that it? I strip for the suckers and that makes me not good enough for a crumby store operator?"

"Maybe that's it, doll. Maybe you're not good enough for me. You might not be good enough for hardly anybody." He crossed to the vacated bunk and lay on it. "Now, take it out of here and peddle it somewhere else."

The redheaded girl glared at him venomously and rushed out of the trailer.

He watched her go, then began cursing himself as soon as the door slammed behind her. Why? Why insult the girl? All she tried to do was set up a relationship for the season. To combat loneliness and boredom. To get a little protection from a man. Who in hell was he to be choosy about a stripper? He drank deeply from the glass and looked drunkenly around the trailer. His eyes came to rest on a typewriter case in one corner. It was dust-covered. He squinted, examined it owlishly. Oh, yeah. Have to try that sometime. They said you could do it. Braden could write, had something to say. Just put it down one word after another and you'd be able to . . . He let his head fall to the pillow. The ceiling went around and around, shutting out all sound, all sight—a humming vortex sucking him upward.

An insistent knocking battered through his semiconsciousness, forcing him to open his eyes. He shut them again quickly. The trailer lights drove through the lids, into an aching head, and he tried to turn over. The knocking continued. Finally, he struggled to a sitting position. He swung his legs to the side of the bunk and rose slowly on unsteady legs.

"All right!" he croaked. "I'm coming!" He walked to the door and opened it.

The man stood in the square of light just outside the door. He looked up at Braden, smiled and waited for recognition. He was a solid man, somewhat past middle-age, conservatively and expensively attired. Braden gazed at him, weaved slightly, then leaned forward.

"I don't believe it!" He swayed, then stepped back from the door. The man entered the trailer and spoke quietly.

"Hello, Stanley."

"Clay?" Braden peered closely at his visitor. "Clayton Ashe?"

The older man nodded and extended a hand.

"Well, I'll be damned!" Braden shook the man's hand, then moved farther back into the trailer. "Sit down, Clay, sit down." He indicated the chair. "It's been almost fifteen years, boy. Fifteen years. What in . . ." He broke off and looked down at himself wryly. "Let me pour some water over my head and maybe I'll make more sense. I'll make us some coffee, too, if you can stand that instant stuff." He turned on the electric stove, then glanced at his watch and shook his head. "Hell, I was only out for thirty minutes. No wonder I'm still half-loaded."

"Would you rather I returned in the morning?" Ashe asked. "I had to take a cab out here and I didn't think it would take me so long to locate you. If you—"

"Nope. Just sit there on the chair. I'll be with you in a minute."

Ashe sat quietly while Braden cleaned himself up. He looked around the untidy trailer but made no comment. Braden finished, then looked in the top of the now-steaming container of water. He placed cups and a jar of powdered coffee on a trunk top. His movements were stiff, still alcohol-sloppy.

"I've seen your name mentioned from time to time on the sports pages, Stanley," Ashe volunteered diffidently. "When you were handling race horses."

"I made the papers once in a while." Braden prepared the coffee, handed Ashe a cup and took one himself. He leaned against the side of the vehicle and studied the older man. "Now, what in hell are you doing out here?"

"Looking for you."

"You're kidding."

"No," the man said seriously, "I'm not joking. I flew in to Coeur d'Alene this morning, rode a bus to this little town, then took a taxi out here to the carnival grounds."

"Yeah, but how'd you know I was with a show? With this one, up here in Idaho?"

"It wasn't easy. I remembered you were with a carnival before you began booking horses, so I consulted a *Billboard* magazine. It listed four or five shows working the West, so

I began looking through them, one by one. Yesterday, a man on one of the Kraft shows said he'd heard you were with this carnival. I came up here, inquired on the lot, and here I am."

Braden nodded. "Then this must be a lot more than a social call, Clay." He looked at Ashe. "If you went to that much trouble, you must want me for something. Right?"

"Yes. I'm in trouble and I need your help." The man leaned forward. "I need it badly."

"From here?" Braden gave a short laugh. "This is the end of the line. A couple of years ago I could have done you some good. But now?" He gestured around the trailer. "You can see how I'm living."

Ashe leaned back in his chair. "It's much larger than the cell, Stanley."

Braden reached for a cigarette and lit it, then sipped some of the hot coffee. Finally he answered. "Yeah. It's damned near twice as big." He paused for a moment. "Whatever it is, you think I can help, huh?"

"I hope you can. Will you listen?"

Braden moved to the bunk and sat on the edge. "Spill it."

"I guess it starts back in the cell." Ashe settled into a storytelling position, one arm thrown over the back of his chair. "When I left prison fifteen years ago, I couldn't go back into the brokerage business." He glanced at Braden. "You know that, and you know why."

"I know. Go ahead."

"I moved out to California and started buying up small parcels of land. I had that much money left and I thought it would be a good long-term investment. As it turned out, it proved to be much better than that. I've been able to subdivide and build. Some of it, I contract-leased. And I've done quite well."

"The trouble," Braden said impatiently.

"I'm getting to that. I have to fill you in on all of it before you can understand my position." Ashe cleared his throat and continued. "If you remember, I had a wife and a small daughter waiting when I left prison."

"I remember."

"My wife passed away about five years ago, and I've finished raising the girl myself." He looked at Braden, eyes tightening at the corners. "It seems I've done a poor job of it."

"Why?"

Ashe hesitated a moment, then let it come out. "She's disappeared."

Braden remained silent for a moment, then asked: "Why not call in the law, Clay? You're clean, aren't you?"

"Of course." Ashe put both hands on his knees. "For fifteen years. But I can't call in the police on this thing. I can't. Not with my background. I couldn't stand the publicity if it came out. Also, I'm reasonably certain she hasn't been kidnaped or held against her will. People I know think they've seen her around Bel-Air and North Hollywood, and I—"

"How do you figure she's disappeared?" Braden interrupted.

"She left our home in Santa Barbara about eighteen months ago, but kept in touch with me for a time. She sent home for some of her things a couple of times and asked for money now and then. Then, about ten months ago, she dropped out of sight. Completely, as far as I was concerned."

"You've checked everything?"

"Oh, yes. Hospitals, morgues, things like that. Nothing."

"How about her friends?"

"None of them that I've contacted has seen her."

"You're living in Santa Barbara?"

"Yes."

"What makes you think I can help? There must be a number of people who could—"

The older man shook his head. "I couldn't send just anyone, Stanley. I'm not sure of what they'd find. Before my daughter dropped from sight, I'd heard she was running around with a pretty rough crowd. I need someone to go down there, find her, and bring her out. Out of whatever she may be in."

"Bring her?"

"Yes. During the time I was still in touch with her I asked her to come home. She refused."

"How old is this girl?"

"Twenty-one. Almost twenty-two."

"Then how in hell do you expect to force her? She's of age. She can tell you to stick it, and there's nothing you can do about it."

"As I said, she's already refused." Ashe looked up. "That's why I need you. I'm almost sure she's in some sort of trouble. She was seen at some questionable places, and the last time I spoke with her over the telephone she seemed distraught."

"Any good private inves—"

"No!" Ashe said sharply. "No police, private investigators or publicity."

"But why me?" Braden scowled.

"Because you know how to move in that kind of a situation. I certainly don't. Neither do any of my friends. We'd be lost in five minutes. No one would talk to us. You're the only man I know personally who can do it. That's why I took the trouble to find you."

Braden rose, refilled the coffee cups, then resumed his seat. "Why won't she come home, Clay?"

Ashe smiled bitterly. "I thought you'd get around to that eventually." He rested his cup on one knee. "She hates me, Stanley. She thinks I've ruined her life, and maybe she's right. She's trying to destroy herself, I believe, and I want you to find her and bring her home before that happens." He hesitated and looked around the trailer again. "I take it you'd like to get out of here."

Braden just looked at him.

"Very well," Ashe said. "You find my girl and bring her back, and you can just about name your price. I'll put you back in business."

Braden leaned forward. "I still have seven grand to pay off before I can operate."

"I'll pay it."

"What about a bankroll to start booking?"

"I can loan you any reasonable amount."

Braden gulped coffee. "All right, Clay. I'll deal. For those wages I'll find your kid if she's in west hell."

CHAPTER **2**

AT NINE o'clock the following morning the bags were packed. Braden looked around the trailer. By this time Ashe should be on his way back from town with plane reservations for them both. They had talked all night. Mostly about the girl, speculating on possibilities.

"What did you do to her?" Braden had asked.

"Plenty, I suppose." Ashe ran nervous fingers through thinning white hair. "My wife and I didn't tell her anything about the two years on McNeil Island. She was so small when it happened, we didn't think it necessary. We should have told her."

"Someone else did?"

"Yes. I don't know who, and it doesn't matter very much now."

"Did you tell her why you were up there?"

"I tried to. How can you tell a girl that her father went to a Federal penitentiary because he was stupid?"

"Yeah. You were an accidental."

"A what?"

"An accidental. Most of you guys that got mixed up with corporate laws, taxes, stuff like that. Hustlers up there could never figure it. You never became real convicts. All you did was your time, then got out. I used to wonder if you knew you were really up there."

"I knew." Ashe half-smiled. "I knew, all right. I just was unable to identify with most of the men there." He looked up. "You and I got along well, didn't we?"

Braden remained silent for a moment. McNeil Island. He thought fleetingly of the twenty months on windswept Puget Sound. A youngster tossed into an unknown situation, among men who were looking for pupils. A housing officer, with more insight than he was given credit for, had pulled the right card when he housed young Stan Braden with Clayton Ashe.

Sixteen months with Ashe, who never presumed, never condescended; instead put bits of information in the way of the younger man; talked to him about places and things, books and music, fundamentals. And never once preached. He opened so many new vistas, the boy had no time for shivs and gangs, hostility or recalcitrance. Maybe if Ashe had gotten out first, he . . .

"Well, didn't we?" Ashe broke into his reminiscence.

"Oh! Yeah, Clay, I guess we did. You did your own time, took care of your job and didn't run to the man. That's about all a person can expect in any prison." He leaned forward on the bunk. "You still haven't told me the whole story about your daughter."

"She was at school when she heard about it. A senior. She was very close to taking her degree and was the president of her sorority." Ashe paused, went on slowly. "It must have been quite a shock. I imagine she felt honor bound to do something about it, because she left the sorority house immediately."

"Did she tell the other girls why she was leaving?"

"No. Just a short note resigning her office and informing them she no longer considered herself a member," Ashe said, then added: "To us it might seem unimportant, but it must have hurt Carol deeply. She left school entirely and came home."

"Did you and she have a battle?"

Ashe shook his head. "No battle. Just silence. Then one day she asked me if I'd finance an apartment in the Los Angeles area." He shrugged. "What could I do?"

"When was this?"

"About eighteen months ago. You know the rest. Nearly ten months ago she gave up her apartment and moved in with another girl. A part-time actress." He stopped.

"Since then?"

"Nothing. I managed to get the name and address of the girl she moved in with."

"How?"

"From a dress shop. Carol opened an account there and gave them the address of the new roommate."

"The roommate also had an account at the same store?"

"Yes. That's how I got her name."

"How'd you find the dress shop?"

"I went to the Credit Bureau. My daughter had a Chargaplate, and all of her accounts were listed at their office."

Braden nodded.

Ashe pulled a small notebook from an inside coat pocket, referred to it. "The girl's name is Dean. Lila Dean." He looked at Braden. "I'll make all information available to you when we reach Santa Barbara."

"How about a picture of your daughter?"

Ashe extracted a picture from his billfold and handed it to Braden, who looked at it but didn't comment. He placed it in his wallet. They settled down to general talk for the rest of the night. There wasn't much of it left.

"Stanley?" It was Ashe, back from town. He entered the trailer.

Braden leaned on one of the bags and clicked the lock shut. "How'd you make out?" he asked.

"Fine. We have a noon flight out of Coeur d'Alene. We'll be in Santa Barbara sometime tonight. That is, if we can get from here to the airport in time. It's thirty miles from here."

"We'll make it," Braden said. "I just sent for a guy." He strapped the bag, then placed it alongside of the others on the floor. He caught sight of Eddie Bowers through the trailer window and went to the door. "Morning, Eddie. Sorry to bother you, but I need a little help."

A lanky young man came through the door. His hair was tousled, and he blinked sleepily. "What you want, Stan? I just got up," he added unnecessarily. He paid no attention to Ashe.

"You still going to take over that wheel?" Braden asked.

"I was thinking about it. Just as soon as—"

"Forget it. Run down to Nick's trailer and tell him you're taking my store for the rest of the season. Tell him you'll work the same deal I have."

"Sure." The man's eyes darted toward Ashe, then swung back to Braden. "Where are you—"

"None of your business, Eddie. Go see Nick and tell him. Borrow the pickup and come back. You got to drive us to Coeur d'Alene this morning. Tell Nick I said to let you use the pickup to haul this trailer. That's what I do. He'll go for it. You'll be making him a buck." He paused, lips twisted. "You fell into it, Eddie. You can have what prizes I have in the booth and use this trailer all season. Maybe another bonus, too. The redhead from the strip joint. She's looking."

"Dolores?"

"Yeah. Don't tell her I sent you."

The man hurried off, and Braden sat on the chair. He watched as Ashe sat down on the bunk. The older man looked worn and tired.

"So. Now we wait," Braden said.

Ashe nodded, then indicated the entire carnival with a wave of his hand. "How did this happen, Stanley?"

"It's a story." Braden leaned back in the chair. "The last year I operated as a bookie, I was a lay-off man. Didn't take any regular bets myself, just bets from the other bookies when the action got too heavy for them or too much was bet on any one race. They dumped a load on me one afternoon." He reached for a cigarette. "Their calls came in real fast and kept all of my four phones busy. When I finally tumbled to how much money was being called in on this one race, I decided to do some laying-off myself." He looked over at Ashe. "That was when the phones went dead. All four. You can figure the rest, huh?"

"The horse came in?"

"Like an express train. When they called the winner, I was

out of business." He shrugged. "Worse. I owed twelve grand. I've already paid back five of that."

"Are the winners pressing you?"

"No. They were paid. I borrowed enough from one man to pay it all off. As I said, I've already paid him five, and with the interest he's asking, he'll wait for the rest. Not too long, but he'll wait."

"Do you think you were ruined deliberately?"

"I could have been. Hell, I had to be. Whoever gimmicked the phones knew what he was doing. Service came back on about an hour after the race." He paused. "The telephone company never found anything."

"Enemies?"

"I don't think I had any particular enemies. Maybe I was getting too big for some of the people in the territory to stomach, although I couldn't have been hurting any of them very much." He frowned. "None of it made much sense, but I wound up broke. I lost everything."

"The last time I saw your name mentioned in the papers, I believe you were at Hialeah. You had a horse down there—"

"Two," Braden broke in. "Two good horses, a very fancy girl, a house in Brentwood, and an apartment near my action. It took me a long time to get all that, only two minutes to blow it." He stood up restlessly. "Let's get some air, Clay."

The two men left the trailer and walked slowly toward the closed midway. A few ride-boys were working on their ornately painted vehicles, and the generator truck still hummed. The rest of the carnival was quiet—asleep, or out of sight in tents or trailers.

"Were you in this business long? Before you started booking horses?" Ashe asked.

"Not long. I looked up Step Halvorsen when I left McNeil Island and joined the show he was with. I played the tank towns until I had enough to open a booth for myself. Then the army got me for a couple of years with the occupation forces in Germany. By the time I got out of the service, I had enough money to start with the horses."

Ashe nodded. "You used to say that's what you wanted."

"You can damned well bet that's what I wanted. I had it, too." Braden stopped and looked around the lot. "You know what? I'll get it again. I'm never coming back to this lousy lot. Or any other lot," he added bitterly. He turned to Ashe. "Let's get the hell out of here, Clay. Eddie should be back by now."

Two days later Braden checked into the Hollywood Roosevelt Hotel.

A full day and night at Ashe's home in Santa Barbara saw his wardrobe cleaned and pressed, himself rested. Ashe had agreed to pay off his debt of seven thousand dollars and loan him fifteen thousand for a new start. He had expense money and the promise of more when needed.

"This is damned near impossible, you know," he'd told Ashe. "A person can get lost in one of the Los Angeles suburbs or neighborhoods. Spend a whole lifetime there without detection. All I have to go on is a couple of names."

"Bring her back, Stanley," Ashe had said. "If you can't do that, find her and see what she's doing. See if she's all right. I just want her safe."

He would try. He put his things away in the hotel room and left the building. Hollywood Boulevard was busy. Traffic and people, color and noise. Braden turned at Vine. A moment later he entered a building and took an elevator to the tenth floor. He walked into an office.

"Who shall I say is calling, sir?"

A new girl graced the small reception room. She gazed up at Stan Braden, a small frown creasing her forehead. He looked at her until she began to blush.

"Tell Mario it's Braden," he said, finally.

"May I ask the nature of your business, Mr. Braden?"

He shook his head.

"I'm supposed to ask—" She stopped, bit her lip. Then jumped up and went into the inner office, face flaming. Two minutes later she was back. "You're to go right in," she snapped, brown eyes flashing. "He will see you."

"You're a doll," he murmured and slid by the desk, grinning at her. It wasn't right but it was good practice . . . and she was so square. He was still smiling as he shook hands with Mario D'Angelo.

"How's the barrister business, Mario?"

"I'm eating." The dark young man smiled briefly. He had a thin face and small bones, intelligent eyes, and good hair, carefully brushed. He folded his arms and rocked back on his feet. "Well?"

"I've got a job, Mario."

"I don't believe it."

"Yes, I have. A job." Braden sat on the edge of the lawyer's desk. "If I do it right, I'll have enough money to start in business again."

"You call it a business?"

"I think it is." Braden pulled a cigarette from his shirt pocket. "I need to know a few things."

"Look, Stan," the lawyer said. "I've told you this before. Mario D'Angelo, attorney-at-law. But not criminal law. My work is civil and when in hell will you remember it?"

"So who's a criminal?"

"All right." The attorney sat down in his chair, swiveled until he faced the window. He placed his feet on the sill. "I'm listening. What's this job?"

Braden hesitated a moment, then said diffidently, "I think maybe I have to kidnap a girl."

The chair didn't move, nor did the top of D'Angelo's head. Braden waited a moment, tried again.

"I said, I think I have to—"

"I heard it!" The attorney swung around, looked at Braden bleakly. "You think you made a funny?" He waited. "I don't."

Braden grimaced. "You're right. It isn't funny, and I don't like it very much." He looked down at D'Angelo. "Tell me how much I can get away with."

"Get away with how, for Christ's sake? You can't kidnap anyone without going to jail, if that's what you mean. What the hell is with you, Braden?"

"I told you. I got a job. I'm going to do it. I might—you get that?—might step on some toes. I want to know how hard I can tromp."

"Why should I mix in it?"

"Because I want you to, I guess."

The smaller man looked at Braden for a moment, then sighed. "Okay, Stan. Tell me about it."

Braden told him of Ashe's visit and what it entailed. D'Angelo didn't interrupt, waited until he'd finished.

"You want my opinion?" he asked, when Braden was through.

"Certainly I want your opinion."

"Drop it. Drop it right here." The attorney stood up, then walked to water cooler. He pulled a paper cup from the holder. "You're buying more trouble than you can handle. If the Ashe girl won't move, and you try to make her move, you're the patsy in the deal."

"I had an idea that's the way it was."

"That's the way it is. First, the girl is no longer a minor." D'Angelo enumerated on his fingers. "Second, her father can't hire you as his agent in a matter of this kind and make it look good. You're both losers and did time together. Third, you've been on the edges of the rackets too long to be popular with the law in this area. They don't like you very much. If the girl blows the whistle and they get a kidnaping or bodily-harm conviction, no man will be able to do the time they'll hand out. There are a few other points, but why go into them?"

Braden nodded, and the lawyer continued.

"You just can't afford it. When you were a kid you tried to steal all the cars in Seattle and peddle them in Canada. Okay. It was a kid stunt and you did the time for it. Since then, you've kept reasonably clean. But the record still stands. If you stumble, they'll crucify you."

"Yeah."

"You need any more reasons?"

"Nope. But I'm going to do it."

"All right, then. I give up." D'Angelo filled the cup, drank the water. Crumpling up the cup, he threw it into a waste-basket. "Goddamn it, I like you. Don't you think I could have loaned you enough money to get started again? Sure I could. It wouldn't have been too easy to get together, but I'd have gotten it. But not to book horses."

"What's wrong with horses?"

"What the hell do you know from horses? You deal in money and people, Stan. Not animals. Look. I go to the track once in a while. In fact, I give a local bookmaker some business. But it isn't my whole life, and I don't make my living at it."

Braden remained silent, and after a moment D'Angelo went on. "What about the writing? You give up on it? In the army they printed damned near everything you wrote."

"Service publications."

"What's the difference? They used your fiction and the words are the same, aren't they?"

"You've made your point." Braden's tone had grown cooler. "You going to do anything for me, Mario?"

The attorney's shoulders slumped and he resumed his seat. "All right," he said wearily. "What exactly do you want me to do?"

"Like you said. L.A. law doesn't like me, and I don't want a rousting."

"You want me standing by with a writ?"

"Yeah. If they get me for anything serious I won't even call you. But if it's only a general-principle roust, I want to know where to find you. In a hurry."

D'Angelo drummed on the desk for a moment, then leaned forward. "I'll do that much. Either call me here or at home. You have the numbers." He pressed a number on his desk. "I'll tell my wife about it. She'll know where to reach me if I'm not home. One thing, though. I expect to leave town for a few days and it might be that I'll leave tonight or tomorrow morning. Got a case up in Salt Lake City. I'll be taking Alice with me, and we might not be back for several days."

"That's all right. It'll take me a few days to get started

on this thing. The way it is now, I'm shooting in the dark." Braden moved from the edge of the desk, walked to the window and looked down on the busy streets below. "How about a retainer?"

"No retainer." The lawyer waved irritably. "If you get out of—" He was interrupted by the door opening. The girl from the outer office came in and walked to the desk. She glanced at Braden coolly, then looked at her boss.

"Yes, Mr. D'Angelo?"

"Jean, this is Stan Braden. He may want to get in touch with someone from this office in a hurry. If he can't contact me, it may be best that he call you." D'Angelo faced Braden. "My secretary, Stan. Jean Webster."

Braden nodded. The girl didn't look at him. She opened her notebook and wrote in it. Then tore out the page and placed it on the desk.

"My name and phone number, Mr. D'Angelo. I'm usually home weekday evenings."

"Thank you, Jean. I'll fill you in on this later."

"Very well, sir. Will there be anything else?"

"No, not now."

"Yes, sir."

Braden followed her with his eyes until the door had closed behind her, then turned to the lawyer.

"Nice legs."

"Very. The rest of her, too. Probably the nicest thing is the way she watches out for the kids when she baby-sits for us."

"Okay, okay. I'm sorry."

The attorney picked up the piece of paper with the secretary's name and telephone number on it and handed it to Braden. Braden placed it in his billfold.

"When do you start looking for this girl?"

Braden consulted his watch. "In about fifteen minutes." He stuck out his hand. "Thanks, Mario."

The lawyer nodded, and the men shook hands. Braden started to leave the office, then hesitated.

"How is Alice, Mario? And the kids?"

"Fine." D'Angelo looked at him steadily. "If you really wanted to find out, she'd be glad to welcome you at the house."

Braden left the office. He passed behind the stiff-backed secretary on his way through the reception room. She was typing and didn't look up. He turned the knob of the hall door, opened it slightly and looked back at the girl. The rhythm of her machine faltered, stumbled, stopped. Braden just looked, deadpan.

The blush started somewhere below the modest neckline of her office dress, moved up redly and rapidly. She finally looked up, eyes furious, fists clenched in her lap. Braden grinned.

"Are you really home most weekday evenings, doll?"

CHAPTER **3**

BRADEN walked up the west side of Vine Street, turned left on Hollywood Boulevard. Three blocks later he paused and referred to a slip of paper. He looked at a small, single-windowed shop, then walked toward the entrance.

It had a new front of imitation stone with angled, plate-glass window, tinted, and a tiny sign, in unobtrusive gold leaf, placed so close to the door as to be almost invisible. In lower-case letters it named the firm—*perin, inc.* The window contained one model, on which there was one dress. A discreet tag mentioned the asking price of the garment—two hundred and twenty-five dollars.

Inside, he was met by a saleslady. His lips twitched involuntarily as she glided over the carpeted floor. Her heavy, jet hair was carefully and expensively coiffured to expose well-shaped ears, on which hung smart earrings. They tinkled as she moved. She wore a deceptively simple gown, and just enough pancake make-up to showcase a flawless complexion. Flawless under professional lighting. Modulation, too, in the cultured voice, soft and barely questioning.

"Sir?"

"I want to see the boss."

The perfect brows moved skyward by the breadth of one hair. "Madame? I'm afraid that Madame is not at liberty to—"

"Grace Perin." Braden looked at her and smiled. "I want to see Grace Perin. About a girl named Carol Ashe."

The words rattled around the small shop. A customer came in, and the woman's eyes flickered.

"Just a moment, sir. I'll find out if she can see you." She hurried through a curtained exit, returning seconds later with a gray-haired woman. The saleslady went straight to the customer; the other woman came toward Braden.

"I'm Grace Perin. What do you want?" She spoke in a low voice.

"I want to talk with you. About Carol Ashe," Braden said. He studied the woman. This one was different. Fifty, probably. She had a lithe, cared-for body, clothed in a tailored gray suit. Close up, it was evident she accented her hair with a rinse. It was youthfully cut and combed.

"Are you here in an official capacity?" she asked.

"No. Should I be?"

She thought that one over, then nodded toward the curtains. "If you'll follow me, please." She led the way through the opening, past several fitting-cubicles, and into an office. She turned to face him.

"Who are you?"

"My name is Braden. I'm acting for Carol Ashe's father. He's anxious to locate her."

"Are you with the police or a private investigator's office, Mr. Braden?"

"No. Just a friend of her father's."

"I see." The woman eyed him steadily. "I'm afraid I can't help you. Her father was in several months ago and was given her address from our files. Since then I haven't seen Miss Ashe."

"She was a good customer?"

"Excellent." The woman dabbed carefully at her nose with the handkerchief she carried. When she brought it from her face, a small amount of blood was evident on the white fabric.

"Was there any special reason for bringing me back to this office to discuss this?" he asked.

"We don't like to talk about our customers in the shop. It is bad for business."

He nodded, looked at her closely. "Have you any idea where she's living now?"

The woman shook her head. "None."

He reached for a cigarette, then changed his mind. "Was there anyone special she used to come in with?"

"No." The woman looked at him impatiently. "A Miss Lila Dean brought her in to open an account, but I've already made that information available to Mr. Ashe. I really knew very little about her, Mr. Braden. Only that she was a good customer and paid her bills on time." She hesitated. "Does her father think there is something wrong?"

Braden shook his head. "He doesn't know. That's one of the reasons he wishes to locate her. To find out. If you should remember anything that might be of use to me, will you get in touch? I'll be at the Roosevelt."

"Of course."

"Thanks." He turned to go.

"Mr. Braden?"

"Yes?"

"Why isn't Mr. Ashe using official help to find his daughter?"

"He didn't tell me," Braden said, then made his way to the front of the shop. He was frowning as he looked at his watch. It was nearly noon.

He found a cabstand and climbed into a waiting taxi. After consulting the slip of paper again, he leaned forward.

"North Hollywood—1225 Norris."

Braden paid off the driver, then looked at the building. An apartment house. The apartments faced on a large court, second-story doors facing a walkway that extended completely around the inside dimensions of the rectangular building. He found the mailboxes and the apartment number he was looking for. Number twelve. It was located upstairs, near the end of one of the long passages.

He rang the bell. Rang it again, insistently. Finally, the door opened a crack, a form barely visible in the dark interior.

"Who is it?" It was a woman's voice, and sounded sleepy.

"My name's Braden. I want to talk."

"I don't know anyone named Braden. Go away." The door began to close.

"It's about Carol Ashe."

The door stopped moving.

"Her father said she lived here for a while. With you. That is, if you're Lila Dean."

The voice came through the narrow opening. "Wait there two minutes, then come in."

He waited the two minutes, then pushed the door open and entered the darkened apartment.

"Open the blinds," she called out. "Then find a place to sit. I'll be right out."

He did as directed. When seated, he looked about the room. It was feminine. Chintz covers on the chairs, bright pillows on the divan. From his position in an overstuffed chair, he could see a large television set. There were magazines all over the place. Mostly the trades. *Variety* and *The Hollywood Reporter*. Film-industry periodicals.

"Well, Braden?"

A girl stood in the bedroom doorway. She was a blond girl, helped by the drugstore. The hair was piled on top of her head; her face free of make-up. She was clad in a terrycloth robe, held snugly around her middle. The girl walked to the divan and sat down. She tucked bare feet under her and looked at Braden. Lila Dean appeared to be in her early twenties.

"Well," she said again, "do you have a first name?" She reached for a cigarette on a near-by stand, lit it herself.

"Stan."

"Okay, Stan Braden. What's this about Carol?"

"I'm a friend of her father's. He says he can't get to her; can't find her. And he wants her back home."

"Why? She's over twenty-one."

"He's afraid she's in some kind of trouble."

The girl got up and moved to the window. She stood looking down on the quiet residential street.

"Well, Lila?" Braden spoke quietly.

"She could be. In trouble, that is." She turned around. "I don't want to get in any."

"Does that mean something?"

"I don't know," she said sharply. "How come you picked on me, anyway?"

"Ashe had two names. Yours was one of them."

The girl shook her head. "Carol hasn't lived here for over six months."

"We know that. What we don't know is what happened. Why did she leave?" Braden leaned back in his chair. "I'm no damned private eye. All I want is Carol."

"All right. I'll tell you." The girl resumed her seat. "Carol and I started not getting along. Maybe I shouldn't have asked her to move in with me. I don't know. I'm an old tale around here, Braden. Me, and others like me. Had a contract and came all the way out here to find out I didn't have any talent. None. So I began partying around. Nothing too outlandish, but partying just the same. I met Carol on the tail end of a long binge. She was living alone in an apartment and not liking it. So I invited her here."

Braden waited.

"At first we played real hard. Too many drinks and too many nights without sleep. Finally, we got a little help for the hang-overs."

"Barbiturates?"

"Yes." She shrugged. "Then one night a couple of creeps brought us home and introduced us to pot."

"Marijuana," Braden said. He made it a statement.

"Right. Little brown sticks of happy grass. Only not for

me. I bowed out then and there, and the two slobs left. Carol and I had a brawl about it, and she moved out the next day."

"You haven't seen her since?"

"No."

"How about men friends, Lila? She have many?"

"Not while she was here. We had lots of invitations to parties. We usually met men there."

"I'll bet."

"Hold it a minute, Braden." The girl sat up straight and eyed him levelly. "I'm telling you things, and I don't need any cracks."

Braden apologized. "You're right. It's none of my business. Sorry."

"Okay." Her face was flushed. "She had one guy she was interested in, I think," the girl continued. "Anyway, she came in looped one night and called him on the phone. I think she used to meet him once in a while, too."

"What was his name?"

"I'm not sure. Pat or Pete, I think. She never did mention his last name."

"How long ago was this?"

"Just a few days before she left here."

He stood up. "Thanks, Lila." He looked down at her. "How is it you've never run into her since she left?"

"I could say it was a big town, Braden. Maybe that would be good enough, but it isn't the reason."

"No?"

"No. It's easy. I don't go out any more. Not like before, anyway." She smiled crookedly. "I'm working. No talent, but a hell of a body." She stood, pulling the robe closer. "I'm in pictures. Advertising shorts for television. Two more months and I can bail myself out of this rat race and go back to Denver."

"Do you know of anyone else who could help me?"

She shook her head, then stopped.

"Did you think of something?" he asked quickly.

"Maybe. If I can remember where the place was located."

She looked at Braden. "It was real drunk out one night, and we wound up near the ocean. Some big house. A guy at the party came up with a deal to make some sixteen-millimeter movies. All skin, and dirty." She moved toward the door with Braden. "We turned him down, but Carol talked about it some later on."

"She was willing?"

"I don't know. It was just before she moved away from here, and I believe she was getting short of money." Lila reached out and grabbed his arm. "I remember. It was somewhere in the Palos Verdes Estates. We left the party about dawn." She wrinkled her forehead. "I was looking out the back window of a car and I can remember seeing three roosters."

"Three roosters?"

"Yes. Weather vanes. They were on top of a three-car garage. It was very funny at the time, although I can't imagine why. Three roosters on top of a garage." She dropped her hand. "That's all I can come up with."

"It's not much. Maybe if I scratch around enough I'll find something." He put his hand on the doorknob, then looked at her. "You don't have to answer this, but I'm going to ask it anyway."

"Ask."

"Did Carol get together with her dates?"

"She was no virgin, if that's what you're trying to ask," the girl said, amused. "Her father doesn't think he's protecting her lily-white body, does he?"

Braden shrugged. "Probably. That's what a father would think, isn't it?"

The girl's lips tightened. "Yes, I guess it is." She looked up, eyes meeting his. "I hope you find her in time. She acted as though she was running away from something. Or someone. What did her father do to her?"

"Nothing much. She's a little mixed up." He opened the door and stepped through. "Oh, yeah. Ashe mentioned she had a car. What kind was it?"

"A Mercedes. White. A real bomb."

His eyebrows raised. "A new one?"

"No. About three years old, I think."

Braden frowned. "You know where she bought it?"

The girl shook her head.

"Okay, Lila. Hope you make it back to Denver."

She stood at the door in bare feet and watched him go.

He walked two blocks before he found a public telephone. He called a cab and had the driver take him to a car rental agency in North Hollywood. After signing the necessary papers and leaving a sizable deposit, he headed for Redondo Beach and ·the Palos Verdes Estates.

The rolling hills making up the Estates were covered with a network of wide, well-kept roads. These, in turn, were covered hourly by a privately maintained patrol service. Braden drove to the small building that housed the patrol-men and their vehicles. There he found a uniformed driver getting ready to climb into a black car. The man walked to the open window of Braden's car.

"Help you, mister?"

"I think you can. I have a friend out here," Braden lied, "and I lost his address. I was out here once before and remember the house, but I get all tangled up on these roads you have here in the Estates."

"What's his name?".

"Edwards. But that won't help much. He just lives with these people, and I can't think of their name."

"Well, I don't know about—"

"I remember one thing," Braden broke in. "There were three weather vanes on the garage. Three roosters." He pulled a bill from his wallet and tendered it. It was a ten. "I'd sure appreciate it if you could locate the house for me."

The man looked at the bill, then at Braden. "I know where it is, mister." He took the money. "Just follow me."

The house had been ridiculously easy to find. It lay near the center of an acre of landscaped and fenced ground, and was sprawled on the seaward side of a sloping hill. It was a new house, one of many that made up the Estates. Broad picture windows faced the blue Pacific, glinting in the afternoon sun. The terraced grounds were deserted as Braden swung the rented coupe into the broad driveway and coasted to the entry.

He glanced at the three telling weather vanes as he rang the doorbell, then read the small card by the button. He felt as though he should be surprised that the name on the card was familiar.

The door swung open, disclosing a young man in a white coat. A Negro.

"Yes, sir?"

"Take me to Mrs. Perin."

"She's not in, sir. She left for the shop early this morning."

"Then take me to Carol Ashe." A shot in the dark, and how lucky could he get? The man's eyes widened slightly and he started to speak. Another voice broke in from behind him.

"Who is it, Wesley?" A heavy-set man loomed behind the houseman. A towheaded hulk in sports clothes. He peered at Braden over the Negro's white-coated shoulder. "What you want, fella?" Piggish eyes narrowed.

"I want to speak with Carol Ashe."

"Nobody here by that name," the big man said truculently. The houseman had faded out of sight.

Braden looked the man up and down. "Since when do dress-shop owners keep torpedos around? This a new gimmick or something?"

"Look, fella, just move on, huh?" The man punched a huge finger in Braden's chest. "You're on private property so mind your own business, awright?"

"Don't put your hands on me, ape." Braden looked at the finger with distaste. "If Carol Ashe is in this house, I want to—"

The big man thrust out his chin and started through the doorway. Braden hit him. His fingers doubled only halfway, knuckles out, he drove his weight behind a straight right into the man's exposed throat. As the man's hands went up to the throat, Braden sunk a left into his unprotected torso. Twice. Then helped him down with three vicious rabbit punches to the back of the neck. The big man lay on the flagstones, twitching.

Braden looked up in time to see the houseman peering around the edge of the open door.

"What's his name?" Braden asked.

"Borg. Dutch Borg."

"You're Wesley?"

"Yes, sir."

"Is Carol Ashe here?"

The houseman looked down at the sprawled figure, then at Braden. "You heard what the man said."

Braden nodded, stepped over the stirring Dutch, then moved into the driveway. He paused, turned. "Will you tell me your last name?"

"Pierce."

Braden walked to the car.

CHAPTER 4

HE WAS nearly to Hollywood. If it hadn't been for the blond ape, he might have found out something. The man who'd opened the door might have talked. But not the muscle man. He was loyal, probably; stupid, for sure. If he hadn't come charging up behind that houseman . . . The Negro houseman. Braden's hands grasped the wheel tightly and he quickly looked from one side of the freeway to the other, orienting himself.

He began to slow down, then looked for the Western Avenue descent. Once on Western, he headed back in the direction from which he'd come. He crossed Wilshire, Washington and Adams. He found a night-club landmark and moved to the right lane of traffic.

A block past the night club, he searched for a parking space and found one. He locked the rented car and started walking. In the middle of the block he turned in to a record shop.

The girl that came to wait on him wore flat heels, tailored skirt and a cashmere sweater, no jewelry. She was a Negro girl.

"May I help you, sir?" Golden-brown skin blended with the beige sweater.

"I want to see Jay, please."

"Jay?" She raised her eyebrows questioningly.

"Jay Burris."

"I'm afraid you must have the wrong place, sir. This is the Harmony Record Shop. We don't have anyone by that name working here." She smiled gently. "There's another shop down—"

Braden smiled back at her. "In the back. Jay Burris."

"The back?"

"Yeah. Now trot on back there, and if you see anyone who could be Jay Burris, ask him if he'll see Stan Braden. Okay?"

The girl studied him a moment, the smile never leaving her face. "You did say Braden, didn't you?"

He nodded, and the girl left. She walked to a door in the rear of the shop, opened it and passed through.

She was back almost immediately, beckoning to him. He followed her through the door, down a short passage, through another door into an office.

"Hey, Stan!" A man jumped from a chair behind a desk and came over to shake hands. "Where in hell you been?" He was a solid, dark man, business suit covering a sturdy frame. Shorn and barbered to perfection, only a slight scar over each eye gave a hint of a former vocation. He wore heavy-rimmed glasses, a narrow mustache and friendly smile.

"Around, Jay." Braden shook hands, then stood back and admired his host. "You still killing 'em on the Avenue?"

"Naw!" Burris reached out a hand and wrapped it around the girl's slender neck. "I'm ruined, boy. This one held out for the ring and everything. A damned schoolgirl. My wife, Stan. Lucille."

Braden put out his hand. "A pleasure, Mrs. Burris."

"Lucille." She placed her hand in his, then turned to her husband. "He didn't believe me out front."

"Anyone in their right mind would have," Braden said, turning to Burris. "She's a real good one, Jay. She almost had me thinking you'd moved."

The girl laughed, retrieved her hand and turned to go. "See you, Stan. I've got to get back and see the clerks don't steal the store."

The men remained silent until she'd left the room. Then Braden turned to the dark man.

"How old is she, Jay?"

"Nineteen."

"How in hell do they mature so young?"

"I don't know, Stan." Burris shrugged. "Lotsa decisions to make, I guess. Some people have to start early." He walked back to his desk. "What's happening?" He perched on the edge of the desk, motioned for Braden to take an armchair.

"Nothing in your line, Jay. I need some information."

"What kind?"

"I'm not sure."

Burris pursed his lips and looked down at Braden. "Ask me."

"There's a house out in Palos Verdes, and I need to know about the people in it. A guy who works there might be able to give me the information."

Burris began to smile.

"Yes, Jay, he's a Negro. Wesley Pierce."

"He live on the place?"

"I don't know."

"Is it any of my business why you need to know so much about this house?"

Braden told him. When he'd finished, Burris swung one leg back and forth slowly, finally asked:

"You figure this girl's there?"

"Maybe."

"What about her? She want to run home to her father?"

Braden shook his head.

"How you going to make her? Is she three times seven?"

Braden nodded. "That's another problem."

"Damn, boy, you got a tough one. What you getting out of it?"

"Enough to get moving again."

"Oh." Burris didn't pursue it.

"So I need some information. Can you help?"

"Maybe. I'll call around and try to find out who Pierce is, and if he can be talked to. If he's new around L.A. I won't be able to promise anything."

"When will you know?"

"Tomorrow, maybe. Call me."

"Will do, Jay."

Burris looked at his hands, then said quietly. "You need any bread, Stan? I'm holding pretty good, and—"

"Hell, no! I haven't been starving to death."

"All right, all right." Burris held up both hands. "I just asked. How about you and me taking Lucille up the street for a little taste?"

"I'm with you. You're so free with your loot, you buy."

A little over an hour later he parked in the hotel lot, then made for the lobby entrance.

"Mr. Braden?"

Braden looked at the hand on his arm. It was removed immediately. He looked at the rest of the man. A nice, friendly smile, no hat, and sports clothes. Braden sighed. A cop. A handsome, smiling, young and double-tough Hollywood cop.

"I'm Braden," he said shortly.

"Captain Jensen wants to see you, Braden. Now." The plain-clothes man spoke quietly. "You can ride with me."

"A pinch?"

"No. He just wants to talk." The policeman shrugged. "He could make it an arrest."

"Hollywood Station?"

"That's the place."

"Okay, Mac." He looked about the busy street. They

were being noticed about as much as any two businessmen meeting casually. "Let's go."

A few minutes later he arrived at Jensen's office. The captain was alone and he looked up from a pile of papers as Braden was ushered into the room.

"Sit down." He pushed the papers to one side, lit a cigarette and leaned back in his chair. He studied Braden quietly, watched with little expression as his visitor seated himself in a chair by the desk. He was a neat man, dressed in a well-cut business suit. He had light brown hair, flecked with gray. Plain, rimless glasses over calm brown eyes belied the fact that he was a shrewd, tough-minded officer. Braden knew it. The captain spoke again. "I thought we'd lost you, Braden."

"You did."

"Now you're back."

"Just passing through on business, Jensen."

"What sort of business?"

"Personal."

The captain shook his head. "Not good enough. You took lay-off bets in this town. You going to start another action of that kind?"

"Another?"

"All right! I'm not going to argue the point with you. I know what you were, and I know that the bigger boys knocked your ears off. Do you go along with me that far? Just nod your head."

Braden nodded.

"Okay," Jensen said testily, then went on. "As far as I know, you stayed fairly clean during the time you operated in southern California. Nothing heavy. But you've been near the edges."

Braden remained silent.

"I want no operating, Braden. None. I could let you cool awhile for not registering as an ex-felon."

"Don't be polite, Jensen. Say ex-con. It won't hurt my feelings."

"You're still an angry guy, aren't you, Braden?" The detective captain drummed on the desk with slender fingers, finally mashed out his cigarette. "Mario D'Angelo tells me you're the same Braden who wrote some things for *Yank* and the *Stars and Stripes*." He noted the surprised look on Braden's face. "Oh, yes, I know Mario. We're in the same V.F.W. post. A nice guy, and he's your friend."

"I'll go along with that. Mario's a nice guy."

"Why don't you give it up, Braden? Work on a newspaper or something. Write a book."

"Will that keep people from betting on the ponies?"

"No." Jensen looked him over. "You're a pretty clever man, Braden. You know most of the answers, even some of the questions. Well, let me tell you something. You're dodging the responsibility of your actions. And you're doing it rationally and carefully. Sure. Everyone bets on the horses, so what's wrong with offering them a little extra service? Maybe they haven't the time to make it to the track. And if you don't get their dollar, someone else will. Great. But it puts you on one side of the fence and a whole hell of a lot of people on the other. Nice people. Ever meet any?"

Braden looked at him.

"You figure I think a bookie's a bad man?" Jensen continued. "Compared to the guns and strong-arm punks, he's an angel. He doesn't hurt people as a rule, and he puts his money on the line." He leaned forward. "But he's breaking the law! Look. About twelve thousand new people are coming into this state every month. And people away from home get into trouble more often than they do when they're in · their own back yard. We have plenty of problems with these people, and the books don't help matters any. No one on your side helps—no matter how small their operation. It's the wrong side."

"Don't worry about me," Braden said, "or about me operating in your territory. I'm leaving in a few days."

"All right." Jensen looked at him, eyes steely behind the glasses. "You can go, Braden. Don't stub your toe. Don't get involved in anything that makes me want you. You do, and I'll try to see that you're buried."

Braden left the police station and rode a cab to the hotel. In his room he tried to reach D'Angelo at his office, then his home. No answer. He dug out the secretary's number and dialed a Citrus number. The phone clicked.

"Hello?"

"Is this Jean Webster?"

"Yes. Who is this, please?"

"Stan Braden."

"Oh."

"I tried to call Mario. No luck."

"Mr. D'Angelo has gone to Salt Lake City, Mr. Braden." The girl's voice was cool and civil.

"Do you know when he'll be back?"

"No, I don't. He doesn't either, for sure. It may take several days up there. Is there anything else I can do for you?"

"No, I guess not."

"Very well, then. Good-by, Mr. Braden."

Braden looked at the dead receiver and shrugged. So she was mad. Probably figured his wolf act at the office was for real. He got the hotel switchboard operator and put in a call to Clayton Ashe in Santa Barbara. Ashe answered the phone.

"Stanley?"

"Yes."

"Are you all settled down there?"

"All settled."

"Any leads on Carol?"

"Maybe, Clay. What kind of car did she have?"

"A Ford convertible. I bought it for her just before the trouble."

"Well, she's driving a Mercedes now. That particular foreign car comes high. About twelve thousand, new. If it's one of the big ones. Hers is about three years old. It should have cost her around sixty-five hundred. Where would she get that kind of money?"

"I don't have the slightest idea." Ashe sounded worried. "Are you sure it belongs to her?"

"That's what I understand. How much money did you give her?"

"I had the bank send her a check every month. Five hundred."

"Five, huh? Well, she could do all right on that, but she couldn't buy a Mercedes with it. Not for cash, anyway. She didn't have any other money? Of her own?"

"No, Stanley, I'm sure she didn't." Ashe paused, then asked, "What are you going to do now?"

"Keep looking. I'll let you know just as soon as I find out anything." He said good-by and replaced the receiver. He cleaned up and prepared to leave for the hotel dining room. As he was about to leave the room, the phone rang. It was a woman.

"Mr. Braden?" The voice was husky.

"Speaking."

"This is Carol Ashe."

"Carol Ashe?" Braden sank to the bed. "How did you know where I was sta—"

"Never mind." She sounded agitated. "I haven't much time to talk and I must see you. It's terribly important."

"Yes, but—"

"There's a drive-in restaurant on the corner of Los Feliz and Brand Boulevard. In Glendale. Do you know it?"

"I know where it is, but how did—"

"Meet me there at nine. Park in the regular parking area and leave your lights on for a little while. I'll come to your car."

"But—" A click sounded as the connection was broken.

Braden sat on the bed for a few moments, making up his mind. He finally shook his head and rose irritably. He had to go.

Minutes later he was on his way to the suburban city. He looked at his watch. Only seven-forty-five. There was plenty of time to eat before the appointment. Once on Los Feliz, he followed that many-directioned artery into Glendale.

He turned into the parking area of the drive-in. It was located almost at the suburb's southern limits. There were scantily clad car waitresses, an inside dining room, a patio dining room and a cocktail lounge. There was entertainment nightly in the bar. It was a drive-in restaurant, southern California style, and one of many.

Braden avoided the car-hop stations and parked deep in the lot. He left the car and made his way to the lounge. After a couple of before-dinner drinks, he ordered a steak and had it served in one of the booths in the cocktail lounge. At five minutes to nine he returned to his car. Clear, starry skies made deep shadows in the rear of the parking area. He didn't quite get the door of the car open.

There were two of them. Professionals. They didn't come up behind him and press a gun to his back. Not these people. One of them called softly to him from the dark space between two cars and let him see the gun—a forty-five.

"Just don't say anything," the other one said. He was standing near the back of the rented coupe. "Move over here."

Braden moved.

"We're going for a walk," the man with the gun said.

Braden stiffened, looked around quickly. Now the gun was jabbed into his back.

"In case you're wondering if I'll shoot, I will." The soft voice was backed up by a steady pressure. "Now walk."

Braden walked.

CHAPTER 5

THEY took him to a cemetery—probably the fanciest cemetery in all California. One corner of the beautifully landscaped place of interment lay a short three blocks from where they'd picked him up. A dark corner, it was far from the architectural assets of the graveyard: the chapels and towers, the magnificent mausoleums; away from the manicured lawns and walkways. This corner lay well below the patrolled roadways.

"Like I told you. One loud sound and I shoot you."
The little man spoke quietly. He stood in front of Braden,
gun held steadily in his hand. He rocked back and forth
on small feet, gesturing with the automatic.

"Take off your tie."

Braden did as directed.

"Now put your hands behind you."

Braden's eyes darted from side to side, and the muzzle
of the gun tilted a fraction. He put his hands behind him
and they were tightly bound by the second man, a big man,
who said nothing.

The little man stepped close to him. "What you nosing
around about the girl for?"

"Personal reasons."

"People think different. Now, why were you out to the
Perin house?"

"I told you. Personal rea—" He almost went to his knees
as the man behind him sunk a fist into his ribs. He gasped,
then straightened slowly.

"Why?" the little man asked again.

"Kiss my—" He hit the ground this time, a sledging blow
behind the ear driving him the last few feet. As he started
to rise, a stifled scream was forced from his lips as a
pointed toe dug into his kidney. The noise brought the side
of the forty-five alongside his head. He fell on his face. The
two men patiently waited for him to get up.

He spit dirt from his mouth and struggled to his knees,
then to his feet. He could feel the blood begin to run down
the side of his neck and he was beginning to sweat profusely. The little man placed the muzzle of the automatic
squarely between his eyes and let it remain there. It was
cold against his skin.

"They want you out, Braden. That means outta town."
The pistol moved back. The man viciously slapped Braden's
face three times—backhanded blows, with the knuckles of his
free hand. The bound man could feel blood running from
his nose and the corner of his mouth. His hair was grabbed,
and he was jerked even with the little man's face.

"Listen, fella," the man whispered. "We could work on you until you were dead. Understand?"

Braden nodded groggily but managed to speak. "I hear you."

"All right. Then get outta this. We see you again and we start working again. And don't try to remember us. We're just doing a job." The little man motioned to his helper. "Untie him."

When the necktie slipped from his wrists, Braden started to bring his hands around. The man swung the automatic pistol at the same time. He didn't miss.

The ground was cool against his aching head. Twigs and leaves adhered stickily to the blood on his face. He moved gingerly and attempted to push himself up. The effort cost too much, and he lay face downward again while he gathered strength.

He moved his hands over his body, then searched his pockets. The money clip and the billfold hadn't been taken. He turned his head and looked at his watch. It was still running. Twelve-thirty. He tried pushing himself up again and made it this time. He stood on unsteady legs and looked around.

A length of wire fence separated the cemetery from a Glendale thoroughfare visible just below him. Midway down this street the night was brightened by an overhead street lamp. Braden made for it, and when he arrived, glanced down at himself. He hastened to a more shadowy area. The first prowl car that spotted him would pick him up—and he couldn't afford that. Jensen would love it.

He headed for Brand Boulevard, keeping close to buildings and dark places all the way. He avoided the drive-in and his car. Glendale police parked there late at night, waiting for drunken drivers to scream into Brand from Los Feliz.

A signboard gave him temporary refuge. He leaned against the framework in the back and thought about it. Where could he go? The hotel was out. They might want him out of the picture so badly they would check everywhere. That meant he couldn't go to any of his known friends—with the possible exception of Burris—but Burris lived clear across town. Another hotel? He looked down at himself again and scowled. Where in hell could he hole up, get cleaned up? It had to be quick and it had to be safe. Where in Glendale could he— Then he remembered. Jean Webster. D'Angelo's secretary had a Citrus number, and if he remembered correctly, the Citrus exchange covered this general area. Maybe he'd get lucky.

Minutes later he crossed San Fernando Road during a rare moment when trucks and cars weren't rushing by. He saw a familiar green booth near a furniture-store entrance. He ducked into the public phone booth unobserved, closed the hinged door behind him.

The cramped quarters offered little room as he extracted the slip of notepaper from his wallet and pulled the directory to the end of its too short chain. He found a page, studied it closely until he found a name. Jean Webster. The number opposite matched the number on the notepaper.

He walked toward the railroad tracks. They lay south, in the direction of Los Angeles proper. A gleam of light advertised a switchman's shack, and he headed for the small building, opened the door and stepped inside.

"Holy Jesus!" An elderly man looked across the top of a magazine, rose slowly to his feet.

"Yeah, that's right. I had a beef," Braden said.

"You sure did, mister. If the other guy lost, you must've buried him."

Braden smiled, hurting one side of his mouth. "I need to know where a street is located." He named it. "I think it's in the Atwater district. If you can tell me, and not report this, I'll appreciate it."

"Well, now, I don't know—"

"An argument over a woman," Braden said. "I don't want my wife to find out about it. A friend of mine lives out here, and I can get cleaned up at his place. If I can find it."

The old man hesitated, then shrugged his shoulders. "All right. You don't sound bad hurt, so I guess it's okay." He gave Braden specific directions and watched as he left the shack.

Braden followed the tracks and headed for Glendale Boulevard. He crossed it and walked down a tree-lined street in Atwater, a neighborhood community, lying between Glendale and Los Angeles. Four blocks farther on he paused, peered at a street sign and made a right-angle turn. He started looking at house numbers.

The street was dark, most of the house lights out. It was a middle-class street, with neat bungalows set back from well-tended lawns, only the muted roar of a distant city bus marring the complete stillness. Braden crossed many lawns and lit many matches, while praying for no dogs. He finally found the house and mounted the two steps to the porch. After hesitating a moment, he rang the bell.

No one answered. He rang it again, then leaned on it. Nothing. He moved to a corner of the porch and found a chair behind latticed rose climbers. He sat down and placed his throbbing head between his hands.

Someone must be crazy or scared. If Carol Ashe didn't want him around, she could have said so. Why have him worked over? Or *was* it Carol? The Perin woman knew where he'd been staying. He'd told her himself. Whatever it was, it wasn't pretty. Not when they'd insisted he get clear out of the area. He shook his head and got dizzy.

It was after two o'clock in the morning when a car pulled up in front of the house. Braden peered through the climbing rosebush. A girl got out of the car, then leaned in the open door. He could hear her.

"Thank you, Lloyd. It was wonderful. No, please don't bother. You've a long drive home. I'll let myself in. No, Lloyd, I insist! See you soon." She shut the car door, bent down and waved through the window. "Good night! And thanks again." She came up the concrete walk, mounted the steps, and started going through her bag for the door key.

"Hello, Miss Webster."

The girl dropped her bag, whirled. Her mouth flew open.

"Don't scream!" he said quickly and stood up. "This is Braden. I need your help."

She put a hand over her mouth, stared at his shadowy figure. Then she picked up her bag and found the key. She opened the door, reached inside and turned on the porch light. The girl gasped at the sight of him and switched off the light hurriedly.

"What do you want?" she said nervously. "And what happened to you?"

"You think we should discuss it out here?"

"I'm certainly not going to—" She stopped abruptly and looked at him closely. "Are you hurt badly? I mean—"

"I'm dirty, bloody, and can't walk the streets this way."

"Oh." She pushed open the door and moved to one side. "You can come in while I call a doctor."

He entered, and she shut the door and locked it. She checked the blinds, finally turned on a couple of floor lamps. She looked at him again. He was beginning to sway slightly.

"Here. Sit down." She grasped his arm and led him to a large, leather-covered armchair. "I'll call a doctor." She turned to go.

"No doctor."

"What?" She whirled.

"No doctor. He might report it, and I can't afford that. Neither can you. The newspapers in this town would have a ball."

"Then why did you come here?" Her arms were rigid, and she was close to tears. "What kind of trouble are you in now? First you barge into the office and—"

"Forget it." Braden attempted to rise, sank back in the chair. "Give me ten minutes and I'll get the hell out of here."

The girl began unbuttoning her summer coat. She tossed it over the back of a chair, then left the living room for somewhere in the back of the house. She returned a moment later with a bottle and small glass. A whiskey bottle.

"You look as though you need this." She poured an inch of whiskey into the glass and handed it to him.

"Thanks." He drank slowly, emptied the glass. She did it again, and he sipped at the second drink. The girl sat on the edge of a chair and watched him. When he'd finished, he started to rise. She shook her head, stopping him with a raised hand.

"When did it happen?" she asked.

"Couple of hours ago."

"I suppose it had something to do with what you were discussing with Mr. D'Angelo."

He nodded.

"They were looking for you?"

"In the worst way," he said dryly.

"Don't try to be funny, Mr. Braden. You're a client of some kind, and I suppose Mr. D'Angelo would want me to help you." She rose. "I have some first-aid things in the bathroom. Come along. You can get cleaned up, anyway."

"Yeah. Give me a few more minutes here. Okay?"

"Very well." She leaned back in the chair, pulled her dress down over her knees. "Where did it happen?"

"The cemetery."

"The *cemetery?*"

"Yep." He grinned mirthlessly.

"How did you find this house?" she asked.

"I remembered you had a Citrus number. All I had to do was find a directory, hope you were in it, and match the name and number."

She nodded, then asked: "Why did you come here?"

"I figured you might be able to locate Mario, and besides, there was no other place to go. The people who worked on me may look again to see if I took their advice."

"What was that?"

"To get out of town. They'd probably check at my hotel and places where I'm known."

"Who were they, Mr. Braden?"

"I don't know."

"Haven't you any idea?"

"Sure. I got lots of ideas. Only trouble is, none of 'em seem to be any good. Someone set me up for this. Hired a couple of the boys to look me up." He frowned. "A woman called and claimed to be a girl named Carol Ashe. Maybe it was. Anyway, the woman had to be the one that set me up."

"Is that the girl Mr. D'Angelo said you were looking for?"

"Yeah. But I doubt that she made that call. There was no reason for it. All she had to do was tell me to lay off and that's what I'd have to do." He reached in his shirt pocket for a cigarette. "Anyway, I still don't know what I'm going to do now."

"How about another hotel?"

"Like this?" He looked down at himself.

"Wouldn't the police see that you were not bothered?"

"Hah!"

She stood up, lips set. "The bathroom, Mr. Braden. I'll see what I can do."

"Don't do me any favors." He struggled to his feet, stood unsteadily.

"I won't!" she said sharply. She reached out and took his handkerchief from the breast pocket of his dirty coat and handed it to him. "Hold this to your ear. You're bleeding on my rug."

She did a job on him in the bathroom. She pulled off his coat and bloody shirt; looked at the T-shirt and pulled that over his head. He sat on the low bathroom stool as she examined his head and lacerated face.

"What did they hit you with?" she asked. She removed the cap from a bottle of antiseptic, began applying it to the cuts and abrasions on his mouth and cheeks.

"A forty-five," he replied tersely.

"A gun?"

He nodded. "A great big one."

"Hold your head still," she ordered, parting the matted hair and looking at the torn area. "You'll have a couple of good lumps up here, but I don't think the cuts are deep."

"They weren't trying," he mumbled, looking up at her.

Her lips compressed as she dabbed with the soaked cotton. She finished attending to his hurts, pushed his head back and looked closely into his eyes.

"I think you have a concussion."

"Yeah?"

"Yes." She began replacing the first-aid material in the bathroom cabinet. "I took a course once and remember that much. Your eyes don't focus very well and you've received some hard blows on the head."

"That means I've got a concussion?"

"I don't know!" she said angrily, flushing. "You might have."

He rose, reached gropingly for his T-shirt. She took the garment from his hand and looked at him, frowning. "Come with me."

He followed her down a short hallway, into a bedroom. She opened a bureau drawer and placed a pair of pajamas on the bed.

"You'll have to stay here, I suppose."

"Huh?" He peered at her owlishly.

"I'll try to locate Mr. D'Angelo in the morning." The girl moved to the door, paused. "Just go to bed, Mr. Braden."

"Aren't you afraid to have me in the house with you, kid?" He tried to grin.

She looked at him with level brown eyes. "Why should I be afraid, Mr. Braden? There certainly isn't anything about me that could appeal to your sort of man."

"Wait just a minute, now. There's—"

She left the room, shutting the door behind her.

CHAPTER **6**

HE AWOKE slowly, groaning aloud when he tried to turn over. He finally gave it up and let his face press against the pillow. His exposed eye noted the pajama-sleeved arm and the sheeted corner of a bed. He remembered. A moment later he tried it again, rolled over gingerly and sat up. He swung his legs over the side of the bed and looked around.

It was a man's room, with dark furniture and sporting prints decorating the walls. A navy-blue robe was neatly draped over the back of a chair, with slippers lined up beneath it.

Now he could hear noises from the back part of the house. They sounded like kitchen noises: a pan hitting metal, a water tap being turned on and off.

He stood up experimentally, face twisting as a sharp pain dug into his kidney. His head felt big but wasn't hurting actively. He donned the robe, shoving his feet into the slippers. They were too big. His clothes were not in sight. He walked down the hallway and found the bathroom open. A new toothbrush, still in its cellophane wrapper, lay on a small stand. Also, his money clip and money, comb, billfold, watch, cigarettes and keys. He looked at the timepiece. Almost noon. He put his things away in the robe pockets, then examined his face in the mirror.

There was discoloration at the corner of one eye, scratches and abrasions on one side of his face, and two cuts inside his upper lip. A piece of skin was gone from the bridge of his nose. Not too bad. He touched his head and winced. Three lumps, each with a scabbed-over cut, were almost completely hidden by hair. He cleaned up the best he could, then went in search of the girl.

She was in the kitchen, ironing his shirt. She looked up at him when he entered, then continued her work. "How do you feel?" Her voice was low, contained, and she didn't smile.

"I'll live." He let the kitchen door swing shut behind him and stood there. "Thanks for the toothbrush." He studied the girl as she ironed.

She was slender, but the pale yellow dress didn't hide the fact that she possessed curves. Gentle, youngly abrupt curves. It was a summer dress she was wearing, cut square and low, two straps over the shoulders. An ash blonde, her slight tan blended with neatly brushed hair. Her mobile, sensitive mouth was set in concentration over her task.

He moved farther into the room, until he stood in front of the ironing board. "You let me sleep a long time."

She nodded. "You needed it." She looked up from the shirt. "I took your suit to the cleaners. There was quite a lot of blood on it, and he's not sure it will come out. Your shoes are on the back porch. There's a shoeshine outfit back there." She picked up the shirt, placed it on a hanger, then hung it in the open doorway between the kitchen and the porch. "Sit down, Mr. Braden."

He sat on a chrome-legged chair at a chrome-legged breakfast table and watched as she switched on a coffee-maker.

"Just coffee, huh? Nothing to eat."

She didn't answer. Taking two cups and saucers from a cupboard, she placed them on the table, then put a large plate into the oven. She prepared breakfast for him—bacon and eggs, buttered toast, honey and coffee. The toast and honey went on a small side dish, the bacon and eggs on the plate from the oven. She placed it all before him, poured two cups of coffee, and sat down opposite him.

"I never eat breakfast," he said.

"You don't?"

"No." He looked at the food with distaste, ate it all. Over a second cup of coffee he said to her, "You don't chatter much."

"Not much." She sipped at her coffee. "My father used to say he liked to think at breakfast. Guess I'm in the habit of keeping quiet."

"That was his room I was in last night?"

"Yes."

"He's dead?"

"Six months ago," she replied quietly.

Braden was silent for a moment, then asked: "Did you have any luck finding Mario?"

"None. I called Salt Lake City this morning. He and Mrs. D'Angelo are checked in the hotel, but have gone to visit friends for the week end. They aren't expected back until tomorrow night or Monday morning."

"Did you leave a message?"

"No, I didn't." She looked across the table. "Not until I find out what you want to tell him."

"Good girl." He noticed a phone on a corner table. "May I use the phone?"

"Certainly."

He called the hotel, got the room clerk.

"This is Braden. Room 706. Yes. . . . Yes, that's right. I didn't occupy the room last night. Here's what I want you to do. Check me out of the room. Yes. Check me out. Have the bags brought downstairs and hold them there at the desk. . . . Right. I'll send a cab. The driver will settle my bill . . . I know. I'll be happy to pay for today. Just have the bags and the bill ready. Okay? What? Give me that name and number again." He noted a pad and pencil on the table and used them. "Right. I got it." He hung up, looked at the pad and dialed again. A man answered.

"Are you Herndon?" Braden asked.

"Speaking."

"This is Stan Braden. Did you leave a message for me at the Roosevelt?"

"Yes, Braden. I want to talk to you. About Carol Ashe. Where are you now?" The voice was deep.

"Never mind. Who in hell are you, and what do you want?" He glanced at the girl, shrugging his shoulders.

"I won't talk about it over the phone," the man said. "Can you come to Armstrong Motors on Colorado Boulevard? It's between Glendale and Eagle Rock."

"What time?"

"I go on duty there at three this afternoon."

"I'll be there." Braden looked at the pad again. "Your first name's Pete, huh?"

"Right."

"I'll see you."

He held the receiver down, asked the girl if she knew the Yellow Cab number. She did. He dialed it and asked that a cab be dispatched to the house as soon as possible.

He replaced the receiver, grinned crookedly at Jean Webster.

"One more call." He looked in his billfold and found the car rental number. He called them and informed them their car was parked in a drive-in at the corner of Los Feliz Boulevard and Brand Boulevard, in Glendale. Would they please pick it up? Any charges for the extra service could come out of the deposit. Yes, it was locked. Would they be able to open it? Okay. He'd pick up the balance of the deposit as soon as he could. He hung up and resumed his seat at the breakfast table.

"I'll get out of here just as soon as I can get my things from the hotel," he said. "And as soon as I can think of someplace to go."

"You think they'll still be looking for you?" She picked up the dirty dishes and placed them on the sink, then filled their cups with hot coffee and sat down.

"I don't know." Braden shrugged. "As I told you last night, I'm not sure of anything. Only that someone got panicky enough to warn me to get clear out of this area. Whether they'll check on me is something only time will tell."

"Can't you find out any more than that?"

"Maybe. If I get a chance to. There's a guy working on something for me now. I'll call him in a little while." He looked at the girl and saw she was frowning. "What gives?"

She flushed. "I'm wondering how to explain you. The woman next door will probably see you this morning. She'll ask."

"She has nose trouble?"

"Not exactly. But this is a quiet street. Only five houses on this side, and I guess they all knew about my father and me. We've never had guests staying with us."

"Never?"

"No. We only bought this house about a year ago. So he could be near the Glendale Sanitarium. We're from the San Joaquin Valley. Porterville."

Braden was silent for a moment. "You miss him, huh?"

"Yes, I do."

"I figured. His room looks like someone still lived in it."

The girl brushed a lock of hair from her forehead. "I took care of him for eight years, Mr. Braden. Ever since my mother died."

"What did he do?"

"He was a railroad man." She looked at him. "A big man. Like you."

"What was the matter with him?"

"Bright's disease. He suffered a lot. That's why I had few callers. He was too ill."

Braden nodded, watched her quietly. He lit a cigarette, smoked until the girl spoke again.

"It wasn't so bad," she said defensively. "Someone had to take care of him after my mother died."

"Sure." He looked at her, then said abruptly, "He's dead, isn't he?"

"I just told you—" she began.

"Then try forgetting it, kid. And about that old gal next door? Tell her nothing."

"What?"

"That's right. Tell her nothing. You're of age, aren't you?"

"I'm twenty-five years old, Mr. Braden."

"Okay. When I leave here, let her guess a little."

The girl's lips parted reluctantly, uncovered small white teeth. One had a chip at the corner, adding to the small smile. "She'll guess, all right."

"So let her. Start having yourself a ball."

"I'm not sure I'd know how," she said coolly. "Besides, you're in no—"

"You'll never find out if you go out with creeps named Lloyd," he broke in. "Who don't even bring you to your door."

"You have no right—" she began angrily. The doorbell rang, and she jumped to her feet. Braden followed her to the front door. It was the cabdriver.

"I want you to pick up some luggage at the Hollywood Roosevelt," Braden said, when the man had entered the house.

"Yessir." He was a young man, alert.

"You'll have to go into the lobby for the bags. While you're there, pay my bill at the desk. They'll have it ready for you." He dug some money from his billfold. "The name's Braden. Stan Braden."

"I'll take care of it, Mr. Braden."

"You'll have to do one more thing, Mac. Can you tell if you're being tailed?"

"Quick."

"Good. If anyone should put a tail on you, lose it. Don't come back here until you do. Understand?"

The man nodded.

"Okay. Make it back here clean and there's a sawsky waiting."

"Right." The young man grinned and hurried off to his cab.

The girl closed the door and turned to Braden. She was still angry. "You have no right to talk to me like that, Mr. Braden."

"Talk like what?" he asked blandly.

"Lloyd's all right," she said. "He takes me out and he doesn't think that . . ." Her voice trailed off and she glared at him.

"I'll bet he doesn't," Braden said.

"It's none of your business," she said hotly.

"You're right." He started for the kitchen. "Got to make one more call." He looked back and grinned at her. "Don't take it to heart, kid."

He called Burris, found him at the record shop.

"Anything yet, Jay?"

"Not yet. Later today, I think."

"Good."

"What happened to you, man? I called your hotel twice last night. Late."

"Trouble," Braden said, noticing the girl had come into the kitchen.

"Bad?" Burris asked.

"Bad enough. A couple of guys worked my head over. Told me to leave town."

"Were they trying to do you in?"

"No. Just a warning."

"Where are you now?"

"At a friend's." Braden looked over at the girl and winked. She gazed at him stonily.

"All right, Stan. Call me tonight before seven."

"Right." He hung up, then stood for a moment, frowning.

"We might as well sit in the living room, Mr. Braden."

"Huh?" He looked up, saw the girl pushing open the swinging door. "Oh." He followed her into the front room, sat down in the leather armchair. He pulled a cigarette from the robe pocket and lit it.

"What are you going to do?" Jean Webster had taken a seat on the divan, legs tucked under her.

"As soon as my clothes get here, I'll take a cab to downtown Los Angeles. Try and stay out of sight until I can get some more information. The guy I just talked with wants me to call him around six this evening."

"Do you expect any trouble downtown?"

"Who knows? Usually, if you keep moving, no one can come up on you. But you can never be sure. If you stop too long, you're dead. People look at you in hotel lobbies. If you hole up in a room, a bellhop might wonder and ask questions. Same with bartenders. Anyone who knows their way around can usually find you. Especially if you're known at all. It's just a matter of time. A neighborhood is better. That is, if you're off the street. In a home." He shrugged. "What's the difference? If they find me, they find me. Besides, they may not be looking."

"I have a home, Mr. Braden." The girl let herself sink into the back of the divan, regarding him steadily.

"What?"

"You can stay out here today," she said quietly. "I don't want to see anyone hurt." She smiled slightly. "I can't imagine anyone who knows anything about you looking in Atwater. For a suburbanite."

"What about the neighbors? The old gal next door?"

"I'm moving soon. As soon as the real estate agent can get a decent offer for my equity in this place. Anyway, none of them are really close friends. Just nodding acquaintances."

Braden nodded. "Okay, kid, it's a deal. I'll see that you—"

"If you mention money, you can leave now." She stood, started for the kitchen. "I'm going to wash the dishes," she said. "You can wait in here until your bags come." She started again, but turned back. "Mr. Braden?"

"Yeah?"

"What's a *sawsky?*"

"A ten-dollar bill."

She nodded, went into the kitchen.

The cabdriver arrived a half-hour later, informed Braden there'd been no tail. He brought in the bags, collected his fare, his ten dollars, and left. Braden carried the bags into the bedroom he'd used and opened one. He was trying to decide what to wear when there was a knock on the door.

"Come in!"

Jean Webster entered the room, saw what he was doing, and took a pair of men's sunglasses from a bureau drawer and handed them to him.

"Here." Then she looked at the light sharkskin suit he'd picked out and shook her head. She went to a closet and returned with a paneled tweed cardigan. "Wear this," she directed. "The trousers to that suit are all right, but no tie."

He held the glasses and jacket and smiled.

"You don't smile very often, do you?" She moved to the hallway. "Hurry and dress, Mr. Braden. I'll meet you at the side door. I have to get the car out of the garage."

"Car?"

"Certainly." Her eyebrows raised. "I have a car."

"Where are we going?" he asked.

"Shopping." She left the room, and he began dressing.

She was in the car when he emerged from the side door of the house. It was a Ford club coupe. Two years old and looking almost new. She was in the passenger's seat, and Braden hesitated momentarily, then got behind the wheel.

The motor was already running, so he put the car in reverse gear and backed out of the driveway.

When she wasn't consulting her list, she was directing him through Saturday afternoon traffic. Ten minutes from the time they left the house they arrived at a Glendale supermarket.

He followed her around the store, pushing a basket. Shopping completed, they put their packages in the car. The girl turned to him.

"I have some bills to pay. Do you think anyone will notice you in the main part of Glendale?"

"Like this?" he asked, from behind the dark glasses.

A small dimple formed at the corner of her mouth. She handed him her purse, then tucked a hand into the crook of his arm.

"This should make it harder," she said. "You could almost pass for a dutiful husband, and that would throw anyone off the trail."

He walked around town with her as she paid her few accounts, finally winding up at the car again. On the way back to the house he stopped at a liquor store and bought some Scotch, bourbon and cigarettes. It was nearly four o'clock when he pulled into the driveway. He helped her into the house with the groceries and watched as she put them away. She put the liquor in a cupboard, then began preparing vegetables.

"Is it all right if I use your car to go see this guy up in Glendale?"

"Of course, Mr. Braden. Will you be gone long? I'll have dinner ready in an hour or so."

"It shouldn't take long," he said, and left the house.

The lot was filled with sports cars. Foreign. They were in all shapes and sizes. Braden wandered through the Jaguars, Porsches and Mercedes, waiting for a salesman to approach him. A young man came from the back of the lot and walked up to him.

"Yes, sir?"

"Are you Pete Herndon?"

"No, sir. I'll call him." The man headed for the rear of the lot.

Herndon was a big one. He was young, his wheat-white hair worn in an extreme crew cut. The glacial blue eyes were unfriendly. They widened slightly at the sight of Braden's marked face, but the man made no comment about it.

"You're Braden?" he asked.

"That's right." Braden thought he recognized the man and the name, but couldn't remember where.

The big man stood solidly on his feet and eyed Braden directly. "Carol Ashe called me. She says you're bothering her."

"Bothering her? Hell, she's bothering me! How do you suppose I got these—" He started to point to his face, then broke off abruptly. "You sure it was Carol Ashe who called you?"

"I'm sure," Herndon said.

"Yeah? Well, someone who said she was Carol Ashe called me, and—"

"Look, mister," Herndon interrupted, "I don't know anything about that and I don't care." His face was flushed. "Just stay to hell away from the girl and keep out of her business. If I hear of you bothering her again, I'll try to find you. If I do, I'll hurt you. Is that good enough?"

"Why? I'm trying to help this girl. Her father asked me to—"

"I don't care about that," the big man said. "Just stay away—"

"All right!" Braden held up a hand. "So I'll stay away from her. Just calm down a minute. Maybe this girl is in trouble and maybe you know why." He looked around the lot. "Is this where she got the Mercedes?"

The big man said nothing.

"What's with you, Herndon? If Carol is wrapped up in something, we may be able to help each other."

Herndon looked at him, hesitated a second, then shook

his head stubbornly. "Just stay away from her, Braden."
He turned to go.

"Wait a minute! Just a sec—" Braden began, as the man
wheeled, leaving him standing there. He followed the big
man's back with his eyes, then turned and left the lot.

He drove back to the house in Atwater.

The girl was still in the kitchen. She looked up as he
entered. "Did you do any good, Mr. Braden?"

He shook his head. "Not much. I damned well know something is wrong, but I don't know what it is, yet. Maybe
I'll find out tonight."

"Why don't you sit in the front room?" she suggested.
He was leaning against the kitchen table, watching her. "You
can watch TV or play some records."

He tried the cathode tube first and couldn't get by the
cowboys or spacemen. He looked over the shelved record
albums. Pettiford and Shearing, Brubeck and Basie. Next
to these contemporaries were some of the older ones. Brahms
and Beethoven, Schumann and Schubert. Some sweet stuff,
too. He reached for one of these. Excerpts from *La Traviata*,
with Peerce and Albanese. Then he sat in the leather chair,
feet on a tufted ottoman, and let the story of the camellia
lady come through.

When it was over, he remained there, listening to the
sharp, erratic yells of boys playing some unnamed game in
the street. Through it all the insistent rhythm of a lawn
sprinkler was punctuated irregularly by the high whir of a
lawnmower. An occasional car went by, horn warning bicycle
and coaster riders. Feet on roller skates, passing and re-
passing, each divisional crack of the sidewalk accenting the
passage.

"Here."

He opened his eyes and saw the girl standing by the
chair. She held a tall glass in each hand.

"Supper will be ready before long." She handed him a
highball. "I was listening to the music. Your selection surprised me." She sat in one corner of the divan.

"Why should it? The guy's a fool who gambles too much, and the girl was a—"

"That isn't what I meant," the girl said, reddening. "You take everything I say—"

"I know what you meant, kid."

"Jean."

"What?"

"Jean. Not 'kid.' "

"Okay." He drank some of his drink, waved with his other hand at all outdoors. "You have all this racket around here every day?"

"What racket?" Jean Webster looked surprised.

"Listen."

She listened attentively, turned to him.

"Those are just neighborhood noises. I've never paid much attention to them before." She smiled. "You must have heard them all your life. Maybe you're just nervous today."

"Uh, uh." He shook his head. "I've never been in a house like this for more than an hour or so in my whole life. A couple of evenings at Mario's, and that's about it." He leaned back. "From a foster home to a carnival lot. Ten years with a show, then I got lucky. After that, it was way uptown. Hotels, apartments, showplaces. Nothing in between."

"Yes, I suppose that would make a difference." She sipped her highball. "Mr. D'Angelo told me a little about you. He said you and he were in the service together, and that you write."

"Write?" He grimaced. "I wrote some junk in the army. For free. Someday I may take a crack at writing for money. Not now. Not until I'm on my feet. Solid."

"Where did you get the idea about writing?"

"In prison," he said bluntly, looking at her over his glass. "A guy put me wise to books. Good books. After I got out, I had sort of a mentor on the carnival. Guy named Step Halvorsen. He died while I was overseas. Step was a nut on education and culture." Braden grinned twistedly. "He figured it made it easier to deceive the suckers. He made me take courses through the mail and go to night school during the off season."

He thought of Halvorsen. Hustle the mooches, boy. Learn enough to speak their language so you can hustle 'em easy. Only get rough if you're in trouble and can't do it any other way.

Jean Webster sat quietly. Finally she rose and started for the kitchen. "I'm fixing chops. I hope you like them broiled."

"You're the cook," he replied.

They were having coffee when the phone rang. The girl answered it, turning her back as she talked.

". . . I'm sorry, I'm busy this evening. . . . No, not another date, just busy. . . . I said I was sorry, Lloyd. I just can't go. No. . . . Yes, of course. Some other time. . . . All right, Lloyd. Good night."

She returned to the table and sat down, not commenting on the call. When they'd finished their coffee, Braden looked at his watch. He went to the phone and dialed the record shop.

"I got him, boy," Jay Burris said. He had answered the phone himself.

"When can I see him?"

"Tonight. Go out to the house, Stan. I'll have him there about eight-thirty." He gave his home address, and Braden wrote it down on the pad.

"Right. See you then." He hung up, tore off the address, then looked at the girl. "You blew your date, huh?"

"It doesn't matter. He wanted me to go to a drive-in movie. I don't enjoy them much."

"Still, you missed out on the evening on account of me." He scowled. "I have to see a guy. In West Los Angeles. I was going to take a cab, but how about using your car? You can go with me."

"I wouldn't want to be any trouble—" she began.

"Trouble, hell. I think you'll like these people. Anyway it'll crack Jay up to see me with an honest-to-God nice girl." He moved to the table. "Come on, kid. I'll help you out here, then you can get ready. Okay?"

She began clearing the table, but stopped suddenly and turned to him. "What should I wear, Mr. Braden?"

"Wear? Well, you could—" He put back his head and laughed. "How in hell do I know what you should wear? We're just going over to a guy's house." He eyed her judiciously for a moment, then grinned crookedly. "I'll tell you what. You put on something you think might appeal to my sort of man."

CHAPTER **7**

BRADEN made the circular turn off Crenshaw, passed the Liemert Park Theater, then headed east on Santa Barbara Street. At Cimarron he turned right, began looking. Halfway down the long, palm-lined block, he pulled to the curb and stopped.

The house looked as though it had been built in the mid-thirties. It was two-storied and had been completely redecorated outside. This was a substantial and spacious home, and Braden knew the story. As the inevitable brown tide moved westward from teeming downtown Los Angeles, some white owners had sold their homes and moved. Negroes with money had bought these houses, on streets like Cimarron, made them new again, then settled in solidly to stay.

Lucille Burris answered the door. She smiled at Braden, looking with concern at the dark glasses and bruised face. Her smile deepened as he introduced Jean Webster.

"Jay's upstairs, but he'll be right down," she said, leading the way to the living room and seating them on one of the two divans that were angled in front of a fireplace. "Scotch or bourbon, Miss Webster?" She moved to a portable bar that ranged along one wall.

"Bourbon, please."

"How about you, Stan?"

"The same." He leaned back and watched his hostess as she made the drinks. She wore a soft gray dress—jersey, he guessed—full in the skirt, the top off the shoulders. Her feet were in ballerina slippers. She wore only her wedding ring and a heart-shaped locket for jewelry. The latter, suspended from a yellow gold chain, nestled against dusky skin made velvety in the indirectly lit room. Almost a costume, and she wore it well. He shot a glance at Jean, saw she was looking admiringly about the room.

"We hired a decorator," the Negro girl explained, handing them their drinks. She took her own, placed a fourth on the coffee table that lay between the two divans, then sat down, facing them. "Jay and I started out with our own ideas, but ran into trouble. We—"

She was interrupted by Jay Burris. He came into the room, shook hands with Braden, smiled formally at Jean Webster and said he didn't believe Stan Braden could have found such a pretty girl—in the caves he usually frequented, that is. He picked up his drink and sat on the arm of one of the divans, next to his wife.

"They did you up pretty good," he said, looking at Braden's marked face. "How's your head?"

"Stopped aching. When do you expect Pierce?"

Burris looked at his watch. "Any time, now. He uses a small club on Broadway for playing purposes. Near Vernon. As soon as he shows, a friend of mine will drive him out here."

"Good."

"You think he'll be able to help you?"

"Maybe. I want to know what—" He stopped, noting that Lucille and Jean were slipping out of the room. "Just what the hell is it with women?" he asked. "Every time they get in a strange house they got to make like building inspectors."

Burris grinned. "It's a disease, boy."

"Yeah. Well, like I was saying, I want—" This time it was the front-door chimes. Burris went to answer them.

Braden could hear low mumbles coming from the entry, and soon Burris returned with Wesley Pierce.

He walked over and shook hands. "Small world."

"Thanks for coming by, Pierce."

"Jay says you're all right, and that's good enough for me."

Braden nodded. "We can talk, then. What you tell me will stay right here and it may do you some good."

"Gold?"

"Yes, the guy I'm working for will pay. I can let you have a bill tonight if you come up with anything. Maybe some more later."

"Ask, man."

"The first thing I—"

Burris stopped him. "You want me in on this, Stan?"

"Sure. You may be able to help."

Burris walked to the bar to make the newcomer a drink, while Pierce and Braden seated themselves.

"How long you worked out there, Wes?" Braden asked.

"About a year."

"You stay on the place?"

The Negro nodded. "Six days a week."

"How many people in the house?"

"Four, including me. Mrs. Perin, Dutch Borg, Carol Ashe and me."

"Carol Ashe?" Braden turned to Burris. "I knew damned well that girl was in the house." He turned back to Pierce. "How are they all connected? Together, I mean?"

"Only one connection, Stan. Dutch and the old lady. They play when Samson isn't around."

"Who's Samson?"

"Somebody." Pierce reached for the drink Burris was handing him. "He gives orders around the place. Tells the girl what to do. I don't know what else he does. I never heard of him before I went to work out there." He took a swallow and settled back.

"Anyone else visit the place?"

"A big woman. Young, and with platinum hair. She only

comes there once in a while. They used to have some frantic parties out there. Big enough so I'd have to get extra help. No more. Not since that Carol girl arrived."

"What about her?"

"I don't know." Pierce shrugged. "She's all right with me. Stays in her room a lot. You want me to tell you what I've put together?"

"All of it," Braden said.

"This is just from parts of conversations. I don't hang around 'em when they're talking and I don't listen very loud." Pierce grinned, glancing at Burris.

"The girl is in something. She doesn't like Samson or any of the rest of 'em very much. I'm the only one she talks to decent. Samson's sending her down to Mexico tomorrow, to a little town just below the border. Ensenada. He had her call up a girl from the school she used to go to and invite her along."

"Did the girl accept?"

"Yeah. Carol called her this afternoon. They have to get back by Wednesday night though, 'cause the other chick's catching a flight to New York on Thursday morning."

"Why Ensenada?"

Pierce shook his head. "I don't know. They were in the patio talking, and I only heard part of it. She's going to drive down."

"What kind of car?"

"Her own. A white Mercedes."

Braden rose, walked to the fireplace and stood with one arm resting on the shelf above it. He said to Burris, "What do you think, Jay?"

His host shook his head negatively, didn't comment. Braden turned back to Pierce.

"Look, Wes, something's funny about that place. You've noticed it yourself. Now, is there anything else you may have seen? Anything different? Anything that didn't make sense to you?"

Pierce wrinkled his forehead over the highball. He started

to speak, was interrupted by the two girls re-entering the room.

Burris made the necessary introductions, and Braden looked to Pierce again.

"Anything, Wes?"

"Maybe." The houseman gazed at Braden under lowered eyelids. "I found a jeep out there, Stan."

"A jeep?" Braden leaned forward. "You mean what I think you mean?"

"Yeah. This was a couple of weeks ago. I figured someone had dropped it at one of the parties, and it had been lying around. I found it in an upstairs bedroom. On the floor, next to a wastebasket."

"A jeep? In an upstairs bedroom?" Lucille Burris exclaimed. Both she and Jean Webster looked puzzled.

Braden grinned cynically. "Different kind of jeep, kids. This kind is for taking a ride, but not on wheels."

"What is it, Mr. Braden?" Jean asked.

Braden faced her. "It's a little strip of paper about an eighth of an inch wide and an inch or so long. It's usually torn from the end of a dollar bill." He moved to the end of the fireplace. "You see, most narcotic users don't have a regular hypodermic syringe. For one thing, they're too bulky for easy concealment. However, they do have the proper needle, plus an eyedropper. Only trouble is, the open end of the eyedropper is too small for the crown of the needle," he explained. "The crown is the square part made to fit a regular syringe. The two ends can be made to fit, though. The piece of paper, or jeep, is wrapped around the base of the eyedropper like a bushing. Then, they push it into the crown of the needle and they're in business. Using paper from a torn bill is on account of the water used to dilute the narcotic. It's tougher and doesn't get soggy as quick as regular paper." He rubbed his chin reflectively. "You'd never find a jeep lying around unless there's a user of narcotics around somewhere too."

"You think someone out there is—" Jean began.

"Hold it!" Braden turned to Pierce. "Wes, have you ever

watched the Perin woman very closely? You ever notice her handkerchiefs?"

"Why, yeah, now that you mention it. She has a lot of nosebleeds, and her eyes—" Pierce turned to Burris. "By Jesus, Jay! The old woman must sniff cocaine. I wondered about her a few times, but I never figured her for a dope habit."

Braden nodded. "That must be it. If you sniff that stuff often enough, it gives you nosebleeds. Almost every time you do it." He faced Pierce again. "What do you think, Wes? Is she on the needle, too?"

Pierce shrugged. "Who knows? Maybe."

"How about the girl? You ever notice anything?"

"Nope. Not a thing. If anyone is using out there, they're keeping it behind doors."

"Yeah," Braden said, "but it might explain the trip to Ensenada. What time does she leave?"

"I heard Carol tell the girl on the phone. She's supposed to pick her up at nine o'clock tomorrow morning."

Braden moved restlessly along the front of the fireplace, placing his hands in his pockets. He finally stopped, looked at the young houseman. "Anything else?"

Pierce shook his head, then got up. "That drains me, Stan." He looked at Burris. "Will that guy out front drive me back to the club? I got a girl waiting down there."

Burris nodded, and Braden walked over to Pierce. He pulled his billfold from his back pocket, extracted a hundred dollars and handed the money over.

"Thanks, Wes. You may have come up with something."

"Any time, man." Pierce tucked the bills away in a wallet, shook hands with Braden. He turned and bid the girls good-by.

"No chance of you getting in trouble out there, is there?" Braden asked.

"No, suh." Pierce turned back, smiling. "I'm jest a happy cullud boy working in the Pacific sun. I don't bother nobody an' all I ask is that no damned fool messes with—"

"Okay, okay!" Braden grinned. "I believe you." He watched

the two men leave the room, walked over and sat near the girls. Burris returned a moment later.

"So?" he asked, after he'd seated himself.

"I don't know, Jay. I want to get that girl home to her father, but I sure as hell don't want to get into anything that's none of my business."

"I don't think that guy Samson is connected with anyone very big," Burris offered, "or I would have heard of him."

"That's a help, but I still—" Braden looked at the girls. "The hell with it. I'll figure it out later. Right now, let's have a drink. Okay?"

Riding home, Jean was silent during the first ten minutes, then suddenly asked: "Is Jay Burris a bookie, Mr. Braden?"

Braden smiled, looked at the girl sitting in the seat beside him. "On a careful scale, kid. Nothing big or spread out. Why?"

"I like them. Lucille is a very sweet girl. She's taking a degree at U.C.L.A. and helps out in the record shop and she's seeing a doctor Monday to find out if she's pregnant and—"

"Wait a minute!" Braden broke in. "What's all that got to do with whether Burris is a book or not?"

"Does he have to be?" she asked. "With a wife, and a baby on the way?"

"He has to be," Braden said shortly. He was silent for a moment, then explained, "I knew Jay Burris when he was fighting. He wasn't a very good middleweight. He took punishment well, though, and started to fight main events. Saved his money." Braden took time out to pass a cruising motorist. "You ever driven through Watts?" he asked. "That old Negro neighborhood in the southeast section of L.A.?"

The girl said she had.

"Jay was living there. He didn't like it—felt he wasn't getting anywhere. And he was getting tired of taking left hooks. So he started booking horses."

"You helped him," the girl said. "Lucille said so."

He nodded. "I helped him. I had some extra money and

I lent it to him. He needed a few bucks to get in that record shop. He paid me back." He paused a moment, then added: "You know that house we were in tonight? Well, it cost him five thousand more than it would cost you or me. But he's on the move, and he won't ever go back to Watts. Neither will his wife. They figure they owe that much to their kid. If they have one." He waited again. "Any more questions?"

"No." She was silent for several blocks, then offered: "I was never in a colored person's home before."

"And?"

"Nothing. I just thought I'd tell you."

He didn't answer, kept driving. The girl let her head fall back against the seat and gazed from the window at neon lights, sky and stars. She only spoke once more during the ride to her home.

"I had three drinks at their house, Mr. Braden. Big ones. I can feel them, I think."

He let the girl out, put the Ford away and locked the garage. He entered the house through the front door. Jean was nowhere in sight. He looked at his watch. Almost eleven.

The girl came in from the kitchen, carrying two highballs. She handed him one, then sat on the couch.

"You're pushing this a little, aren't you?" He indicated the drinks.

She drank from her glass, ignored his question by asking one of her own. "Did you find out anything important tonight?"

"I think so."

"What?"

"The Ashe girl is probably in trouble. In more trouble than she can handle."

"Can you get her out of it?"

"I don't know." He moved to the armchair, sat down and studied his drink.

"This could get you into a lot of trouble, couldn't it? If you did anything to break the law?"

"Plenty."

"Mr. D'Angelo told me." She drank more of the highball. "He said you've known the girl's father for a long time."

"I have. He's the one who started me on reading. In prison," he said. "That isn't why I'm helping him. He'll pay seven thousand dollars if I get his kid home. Plus a nice big loan to get me started again."

She was silent for a moment, finally asked: "Can you tell me why you were in prison?"

"Sure." He lay back in the chair, crossed his ankles. "I was nineteen years old. At that time I'd spent six years on a carnival lot, from the time I ran away from my foster parents. Six years. Four as a ride-boy, then I got to run a flat-store. I got sick of that quick. Nickel-and-dime action. Then some guy touted me into lifting cars in Seattle, peddling them in Canada." He shook his head. "It didn't work. The Federal Government gave me two years on McNeil Island to figure out why. I met Ashe there." He shrugged. "That's the story."

"What did Mr. Ashe do to get in prison?" she asked.

"Taxes, I think. Or maybe some violation of corporate law that got the government on him. It was real technical. He may have been the fall guy for some corporation. I never asked him for details."

She didn't say anything for a time; she was toying with her drink. Then she scowled and leaned forward on the divan.

"What's a flat-store?" she asked curiously.

"Why, that's a—" He stopped, sat up in the chair. "You ever been to a carnival, kid?"

"Certainly I've been to a carnival. Every year up in Porterville a carnival came to the edge of town, and we—"

"Okay, you've seen a show. Well, you remember the little booths where you could play games for prizes? Drive a nail into a plank, or roll marbles out of a trough? Throw baseballs at wooden milk bottles?"

"Yes. I used to throw—"

"All right," he broke in. "If they gambled for money at those booths, they were flat-stores."

"Oh." She hesitated for a moment. "Is that where you started to gamble?"

"That's the place I started. I learned what I could there by studying the rest of the boys on the midway." He shrugged. "I made a dollar."

"You like gambling?"

"Hell, no! It's hard work. That's why I stopped doing it."

"But I thought—"

"I became a bookmaker. I worked with money at the right odds. I was a cinch to make more money." He leaned back. "I'll make it again. It got me what I wanted."

"Yes, I suppose it did." She shifted her position on the divan, tucked feet under her skirt. They remained silent for a time, then he asked:

"How long have you worked for Mario?"

"A couple of months. After my father died, I began answering ads in the paper. I found Mr. D'Angelo's, and he hired me."

"What are you going to do when you sell the house?"

"Find an apartment, I suppose." She looked down. "There's no reason for me to go back to Porterville. I haven't any relatives up there. There were just the three of us."

"You like being a lawyer's secretary?"

"Oh, I'm not a secretary yet. Just sort of a receptionist. Mr. D'Angelo's going to send me to a good secretarial school, though. Just as soon as I can break a girl in on the desk." She stopped suddenly. "Are you going to try to get that girl out of trouble?"

"I suppose so."

"When will you start?"

"Tomorrow, maybe. I have an idea, but I'll have to sleep on it."

"All right," she said, and got up. "You'd better stay here again. It's late, and you can get started in the morning."

He looked surprised, eyebrows lifted. "Sure. It's your house."

"Good. Will you excuse me, please?" She left, carrying her drink with her.

Braden sat there, nursing his highball. He considered calling Ashe and telling him of the latest development, then changed his mind. No use worrying the man until he knew more about it, or knew if there was anything he could do about it. Crazy, spoiled little bitch. Whatever she was doing, she'd probably say she was only getting her kicks. He'd give her kicks. Right in her upper-class—

"Mr. Braden?"

She stood in the doorway leading to the hall. She had changed to white broadcloth pajamas, short trousers reaching only to tanned calves. Her head was cocked to one side.

"May I talk with you before I go to bed?"

"Like that?"

"Yes." She walked across the room and stood before him, feet slightly apart. "I had a wonderful time today. I haven't had so much fun in years. The people I've met and the way you've told me things. I—" She gazed at him seriously, face flushed. She moved to the side of the chair, sat on the arm, then turned to him. "Would you like to kiss me, Mr. Braden?" She had removed her make-up and smelled clean and fresh. "Would you?"

He reached up and placed both hands on her shoulders. He pulled her from the arm of the chair, then cradled her until the upper part of her body lay across his chest. Her breasts flattened against him, and she gasped at the contact, closed her eyes. He held her that way for a moment, then pushed her back to the arm of the chair.

"No," he said finally. "No, I wouldn't like to kiss you."

CHAPTER **8**

THE next morning he prowled around the kitchen in robe and pajamas. He'd awakened early. He made coffee, then sat at the kitchen table with it and mulled over the situation. He was pouring a third cup when the girl put in an appearance.

"Good morning, Mr. Braden." She walked to the cup-board, reached for a cup and saucer. They rattled as she carried them to the steaming coffeemaker.

"Here." He got up, took the things from her and sat her down in a kitchen chair. She put her head in her hands, elbows on top of the table. He looked at her closely. "I know damned well you didn't drink enough to be hung over." He looked at her again. "Did you?"

She shook her head, winced. "I don't suppose so. I had about six drinks all day long. Four of them were big ones. The ones I had last night. I have never drunk more than two drinks at one time in my life before. Maybe—"

"All right, kid, you're hung over. Just sit there." He went through the refrigerator and cupboards. He placed ice cubes, tomato juice, Worcestershire sauce, Tabasco sauce and the bourbon bottle on the sideboard. She looked at it all, then turned her head away. He searched for the right size glass, found it. A moment later he handed her a tall, red drink.

"Drink it," he ordered. "All of it."

"What is it?" She clutched the glass in one hand, her unbelted robe with the other.

"Never mind." He sat down in a chair opposite her. "I'm not talking to you until you drink it. In five minutes you'll be well. I guarantee it."

It took her a minute to finish the drink, four more to look at him squarely.

"You're right, Mr. Braden. I feel a lot better. Perhaps if you'd fix me—"

"One to a customer. Another, and you'd be started all over again."

"Oh."

Braden got up, filled her cup with steaming coffee, then resumed his seat.

"What are you going to do today?" she asked, sipping the black brew. "Did you figure things out last night?"

"I think so." He ran his hand over the stubble on his face. "I'm going out of town tonight. Before that, I have two things to do. You want to go with me?"

"Yes." She didn't look up.

"All right." He stood up. "Is it all right to use the electric razor? The one on your father's bureau?"

"Of course."

He went to the bedroom, took the shaver from its case, then started for the bathroom. The girl met him as she headed for her room. He stopped her. "Come here," he said.

"What do you—"

"Come here." He put the shaver in a robe pocket. "Please."

She moved in front of him, and he took her by the shoulders. "You remember last night?" he asked.

The girl nodded.

"Then, listen. I broke into your life yesterday—moving pretty fast. You got a little carried away last night."

"I was aware of exactly what I—"

"Were you?" In one swift movement a hand went past the open edges of her robe, under the pajama coat, pressed firmly against her bare back. The other tilted her chin at the same moment. Before she could utter a sound, he kissed her. He felt her lips stiffen under his, her body tense. Then, almost involuntarily, her arms crept around his neck, her lips softened and she strained herself to him.

He let her go abruptly. "Yeah. You were aware, all right." He grunted. "That's what I wanted to do last night. If I had, we'd have both been in there this morning." He jerked a thumb in the direction of her bedroom door, then reached out a hand and placed it on top of her tousled hair. She made no attempt to close the robe over her pajamas—only stared at him with lower lip trembling. "You're waking up to what it's like to be free, kid." He shook his head. "Twenty-five! You're a damned baby. Don't throw yourself away on some jerk, and don't read things into people that may not be there. And for Christ's sake, don't take chances like you did last night. You'll get murdered." He dropped his hand and headed for the bathroom.

She fled to her room. Before he had time to plug in the shaver, he heard things being slammed around in her bedroom. He thought he heard strangled sobs.

An hour later they left the bungalow, a slight redness about the girl's eyes the only indication that she'd been weeping. Braden drove through Sunday traffic, headed for the foreign-car lot. He drove onto the property and stopped in front of the lot shack.

The big man was on the lot. He had a couple in tow, walking them around a black Jaguar. As soon as he spotted Braden, he called another salesman and turned over his customers.

"Well?" He leaned in the car window, eyes narrowed. "I thought I told you—"

"I know what you told me, Herndon," Braden broke in. "And I know why, I think."

The big man blinked, looked uncertain.

"That's right," Braden went on. "I believe I know why you're protecting her, and I have a feeling it's throwing you for a loss." He looked up at Herndon. "I've remembered who you are, too."

"What do you want?" Herndon asked harshly.

"I want to talk. Now."

Herndon looked around the lot, called out: "Bill!"

A man came out of the small lot shack and moved toward them. "Yes, Pete?"

"I'll be across the street if anyone calls for me," Herndon said, turning to Braden. "Park your car. We can talk over coffee." He pointed to a small restaurant and started toward it.

When he'd parked the Ford, Braden and Jean Webster made for the restaurant. They found Herndon in a rear booth. He'd already ordered coffee for them all. Braden introduced the girl, noting that the big man loosened up somewhat in returning her handclasp.

"Haven't I seen you someplace, Mr. Herndon?" the girl asked. "It seems to me . . ." Her eyes widened. "Oh! Pete Herndon. You're the one they call the Hatchet. My father and I used to watch every Sunday when the team was out of town and could be televised here. He said you and Les Richter could keep a whole football team honest."

"He had me in good company, Miss Webster." He was studying Braden's face. "What happened?"

"A couple of guys didn't like the idea of me fooling around Carol Ashe."

"Maybe I don't either," Herndon said coldly.

"Maybe you don't. But I'll tell you this: she's in more trouble than you think, and I may be able to help her. That is, if you'll co-operate."

"What do you want to know?"

"Did you sell her the car she's driving? The white Mercedes?"

"Yes. She saw the car and liked it. I took her Ford in on it. In fact, she still owes payments on the car that I'm just letting ride."

"You went around with her?"

"Some."

"How well do you know her?"

"Is that important?"

"It may be."

"I've got to know more than that, Braden. I don't know you from a—"

Braden broke in. "All right, Herndon, here it is. Her father, Clayton Ashe, wants to find her. He's an old friend, so he called on me. You can call him in Santa Barbara if you want to. Right now, I believe she's in a bad jam and I want to get her out of it. Anything else you need to know?"

"How come her father called on you instead of the law?"

"He seems to think I can get the job done without any publicity."

"I called a couple of guys after you left yesterday. Are you the Stan Braden who has a book?"

"I had a book. No more."

The big man made up his mind, hunched forward. "Okay. I met her almost a year and a half ago. Right after a game." He glanced at Braden. "I play—"

"I've seen you with the Rams," Braden interrupted. "You're one of the three best defensive halfbacks I've ever seen."

Herndon went on, "Well, after this game, I left the Coliseum with a couple of guys. Went to a party. Sorority party. That's where I met her. About six months later I sold her the car, and we started making it pretty steady." He looked across the table at them both. "You understand what I mean? A guy can tell. We were making it real fine."

"I understand," Braden said.

"Two or three months after that she started breaking dates, making excuses. I don't need any truck to fall on me, so I backed off. I had an idea of what she was doing." He shook his head. "I couldn't fight it."

"You haven't seen her since?"

"No. I've talked to her twice over the phone. Yesterday, when she called complaining about your interfering, and once some time ago."

"How long ago?"

"About six months, I guess. The club had just come back from the eastern swing. She was crying. All she did was repeat my name a few times, then hang up." Herndon signaled for the waitress, had their coffee cups refilled. He eyed Braden curiously. "Just why are you so worked up? You don't even know this girl. What's in it for you?"

Braden sighed. There it was. A question repeated millions of times a day—that had to be answered.

"Money, Herndon. Just money."

"It figures." The football player stood up. "I thought you said Carol's father was an old friend," he said coldly.

"He is."

"And you're taking money?"

"I'm taking money," Braden said evenly.

"Okay." Herndon leaned on the table and faced Braden. "If I can help her, I will. But nothing crooked, Braden. No hustler tricks. You don't sound right to me. One little wrinkle out of you and I'll break your leg."

"I think he wants to help her, Mr. Herndon," the girl interjected quietly.

"Or himself," the big man said. "These guys always have to figure a way to make a buck for themselves."

She nodded. "I know. But I think he wants to help this girl. I don't know whether you think anything of her, but—"

"Look!" Braden broke in angrily. "I don't need any help, kid. If this ape is worried about motives, he can go take a . . ." His voice trailed off as he reached for his coffee.

"All right, Braden." Herndon resumed his seat. "This lady sold it. What do you want?"

"Tell him, Mr. Braden." The girl plucked at his sleeve.

Braden settled back, looked at the athlete. "You remember the Mercedes you sold Carol?"

"Every nut and bolt."

"You got another like it?"

"Yes. There are three on the lot right now. We keep—"

"I mean exactly like it. Same color, same upholstery, same model."

"Why do you need the—"

"Look, genius," Braden interrupted, "you want to tell me have you got the car or you want to play Twenty Questions?"

Herndon's face turned red. "Sometime I'll talk to you about your mouth."

"Save it for the Browns. You got a car like that?"

The football player started to make a retort, stopped. "We have one. Hers was a '52 300SL convertible. Tan upholstery. This one's just like it. Off-white with a black nylon top."

"It has matched luggage?"

"Yes."

"Same style?"

"Same style. Pigskin. They come equipped that way."

"You remember what the keys were on?"

"Sure." Herndon looked at Braden, puzzled. "I gave it to her. A short chain with a football on it."

"Got any more?"

"One. For my own car."

"I'll need that, too," Braden said, went on. "Her plates have a bracket?"

"Bel-Air."

"Same brackets, then. How about the registration-slip holder?"

"Plain black. Snap-on type."

"Okay, match it."

"Anything else?" Herndon asked sarcastically.

"Yeah. A plain American sedan. I'll need both cars by this evening."

Herndon pondered it for a moment. "All right, mister. I'm only the manager over there, but I can swing it. You can have 'em. For your sake I hope you're playing it down the middle. How about a '56 Olds for the second car?"

"Good."

"I'll have 'em gassed and waiting for you. How long is this going to take?"

Braden shrugged. "I don't know." He reached for a cigarette, lit it. "If it runs longer than a couple of days, I'll have Jean call you." He indicated the girl, turned back to Herndon. "Does anyone at all know about you and Carol?"

"No."

"How can you be so sure?"

"We never went anywhere we were known." Herndon hesitated a moment. "I was married, Braden. Separated, but the divorce wasn't final. Being on the club and everything, the papers would have given any girl I was with too much publicity. We avoided it."

"I hope you avoided it real good."

"I'd bet," Herndon said, positively.

"Your life?" Braden asked quietly. The big man's eyes widened, and the girl gave a small gasp. "Yeah, that's what I said. If I'm right, it could come to that. If they connect her with you."

Herndon rubbed his jaw with a large hand. "I'm sure. Anyway, I'm pretty hard to hurt."

"You think?" Braden stood, reached out a hand for Jean. "Shoulder pads won't stop a bullet, halfback."

He and Jean left the restaurant, returned to her car.

"May I have a cigarette, please?" They were several blocks from the lot, heading toward Hollywood.

"Sure." He pulled one from his pocket, lit it and handed it to her. "Didn't know you smoked."

"Once in a while." She opened the window on her side, let more of the warm day enter the car. "Is it going to be that dangerous?"

"Probably not."

"You didn't tell Pete Herndon very much."

"No. In my business that gets to be a habit."

She didn't comment at once, just sat watching the city go by the window. Finally she said quietly, "You've told me quite a lot." She turned partially sideways on the seat, sat looking at him.

"Too much," he said shortly.

"I think Pete's in love with that girl."

"Or thinks he is. That's good enough."

"Oh, I think you—" She stopped, bit her lip and looked out of the window again. "Are we going for a ride?"

"Yeah. A long one. Relax and enjoy it."

Braden drove all the way to the ocean. He passed through the center of Santa Monica, turned right at the end of Wilshire Boulevard and drove down to the coast highway. He made a full left turn there and headed for Ocean Park.

The amusement pier was teeming with people, and he had trouble finding a parking lot with a vacancy. He found one behind the Speedway. He turned to Jean Webster.

"I have to look up a guy down here. You'd better wait in the car."

"Why?"

"The place I'm going to is kinda rough."

"I want to go, Mr. Braden."

"All right. Suit yourself."

They walked toward the Speedway, crossed that narrow, misnamed alley, and were soon on the street that served as a midway for the beach concessions.

Braden looked down at the girl's hand. She'd taken his arm. He felt like a square and probably looked like one, he guessed—like the crowds streaming by in both directions, going up one side and down the other, stopping in the hot

sun to eat, play, perspire and be taken, in shirt sleeves and
sun suits, with sticky kids and sore feet. He grimaced, then
hurried the girl through the mass of humanity until they
reached one of the streets running into the midway. He
walked her up this street and into a bar called The Pig.

It was tucked away on a side street, hiding from the general public. A purely functional place of business, with
liquor, bartender and customers. It had a plank between
the last two, and some stools to make it easier, even a
couple of booths, placed at the rear of the pinball machines
and juke box. The narrow room was almost dark.

He escorted the girl to the last of the booths, walked
back to the bar and bought two beers. Booth service in The
Pig was on a carry-it-yourself basis. As they drank, his eyes
began to get accustomed to the cavern light. He studied
the customers at the bar. They were young—every damned
one of 'em too young to be in the place. As usual. He
grunted and put his glass down. With liquor licenses there
was always an angle, always a way.

"Be right back," he said to Jean Webster. He rose and
went to the bar. Moving to an open space, he waited to
catch the bartender's eye. The hum of conversation stopped.
He looked up and down the twenty-foot plank.

They wore leather jackets, in spite of the day, T-shirts,
grimy blue jeans and buckled boots. The boy on his right
looked him up and down. He was a fair-skinned boy with
pale eyes, who may have been seventeen.

"You want something, Dad?" A quiet voice, with little
expression. The boy was acutely conscious of the rest of
the room.

Braden's lips twitched and he turned back to the bar,
looking again to waylay the bartender. He heard a loud
click, turned in time to see the boy cleaning his nails with
the sharp end of a switch-blade knife. The boy didn't look
up as he said evenly, "You get lost off the midway?" Pale
eyes darted to Braden. "I asked a question. How about
an answer, huh?"

The bartender stood with hands on the edge of the bar.

He looked, saying nothing. The kids were money in the bank, so why run 'em out in the street? Braden's eyes flicked his way, narrowed. He sighed and turned. He threw his beer in the boy's face, glass and all.

As the glass left his hand, he jumped forward, twisted the boy quickly and roughly, pinned the knife hand, forcing hand and knife to their owner's throat. All this before the other drinkers could get untracked. They started to move and Braden stopped them with his voice.

"One move!" He pressed the point of the knife to the young throat and felt the body tremble. The boy hadn't uttered a sound. The rest halted. "One lousy move and I cut this punk's head off," he said coldly. He waited.

"Okay." He pried the knife from his captive's hand, pushed him away. He drove the blade in the bar and snapped it off, throwing the pieces to the floor. "I know you're a man, kid. You don't have to prove it." He turned back to the bartender. "I'm going to wait here an hour. If Billy Cash comes in, tell him Stan Braden wants to see him. You expect him?"

"Yeah." The man looked shaken. "He usually comes in about noontime."

Braden nodded, stared at the man steadily. "Someday someone's going to sweep this trap into the street, Mac. Into the gutter—where it belongs." He turned to the boy. "You ought never pull steel, kid—not till you're ready to use it."

No one said a word as he went back to the booth. He sat down, raised his eyebrows at the girl. She'd seen the whole thing over the back of the booth. Jean Webster was speechless.

"I told you you'd better wait in the car."

"Why, those boys are only—"

"Forget it. That's the way it is, and it would take me too long to explain why." He looked up. The bartender was bringing them more beer. "We shouldn't be here long." He looked at his watch. It was ten minutes after twelve.

A few minutes later a deeply tanned boy entered the bar, carrying a white crash helmet under one arm. He was slender and quick-moving. He went to the stools, paused as the bartender called to him, listened, then made his way back to the end booth. He looked at Braden without comment, let his eyes slide to the girl.

"Hello, Billy," Braden said.

"Hello." The boy kept his eyes on Jean. "You need me for something, Braden?"

"Sit down, Billy. Here! On this side."

"Sure." The boy sat down by Braden, eyes still on the girl. "Who's the beetle, Braden?"

"The beetle is Jean Webster." He kept a straight face. "Keep your eyes to yourself, Billy, or I'll belt you."

"Okay." The boy leaned toward the girl. "I'm Billy Cash, baby." He turned to Braden, eyes flat. "You called me. . . . What?"

"You driving?"

"Yeah."

"Today?"

"In a couple of hours. Main event."

Braden nodded. "Your own car, Billy?"

"Hell, no! Who has a car?" The boy reached into a black leather jacket for a cigarette, lit the match on his thumbnail. "I asked what, Braden?"

"You want to make two bills?"

"Doing what?"

"Driving."

"That's all? Nothing heavy?"

"Nothing heavy. You may get a traffic citation. I pay if you do."

"Where do I do this driving?"

"Between here and the border. You won't have to cross over. You'll stop north of Tijuana, at San Ysidro."

"After the races today, huh?"

"Right. We leave tonight. You may be gone until Thursday. I pay expenses."

The boy stood up. "Okay. Where do I see you?"

"Glendale. Armstrong's car lot on Colorado. Foreign cars. You know where it is?"

"I'll find it."

"Good. Eight o'clock."

The boy nodded. He leaned over the table toward Jean Webster. "You know what, girl? You oughta come to the track and watch me drive." He walked away, white helmet in hand.

Braden was a mile up Wilshire Boulevard before the girl mentioned the interview with Billy Cash.

"I saw a Marlon Brando picture about a—"

"Uh, uh," he interrupted. "Wrong vehicle. This kid drives jalopies—and the midgets. No motorcycles."

"The way he looked at me. Just as though he were undressing me."

"That's what he was doing. You can bet on it."

"But he's so young!"

"Billy Cash was never young, kid. His old man was a two-bit operator on a show. I don't think Billy remembers his real mother. One carny woman after another. I guess they did the best they could."

"Has he been with a carnival all his life?"

"Most of it. That, and the beach. I had him running errands for me when he was a little kid. It was about the only way he could get enough dough to eat on. His old man lushed up most of the family money."

The girl shook her head.

"Don't worry about Billy," Braden said. "He's luckier than most of those kids."

"What do you mean?"

"He knows who he is. Billy Cash, race driver. The others are still looking." He shrugged. "Maybe they'll never find out. Not until they get into some real trouble first. I don't think Billy will foul up now. Not anything real bad, anyway."

"What will become of a boy like that—finally?"

He grunted. "You're sitting next to one. What's going to happen to me—finally?" He lit two cigarettes with the car lighter, handed her one.

"No, I'm serious, Mr. Braden. What will happen to him?"

"Kill himself, maybe. On the dirt tracks. If he doesn't, you may hear of him on the bricks."

"The bricks?"

"Indianapolis. World Series for the gas boys. Most of 'em start on the dirt." He looked at the time. "You want to eat somewhere? You could drop me off at the car lot later on."

"I think I'd rather go home."

"Okay."

It was beginning to seem familiar, pulling into the driveway of the small frame house. Inside, Jean went to her room. Braden went into the kitchen and put in a call to Ashe. He found him in.

"Clay?"

"Yes, Stanley."

"I've located her."

"Where?" The older man sounded excited. "Is she all right? Where is—"

"Wait a minute!" Braden waited until the line was quiet, then continued, "I know where she is, but I haven't seen her yet. And I don't think she's all right. I can't explain it over the phone, but I may have to get a little rough. Take some steps. How far do you want me to go?"

"How bad is the trouble?" Ashe asked.

"It can be plenty bad."

"Then go as far as you have to," Ashe said more calmly. "I'll back you just as much as I'm able. Do you need any money?"

"No. I'll call you just as soon as I know anything more." Braden said good-by, went into the living room. He chose a record album and put it on the machine. Then he went back to the kitchen and made himself a drink. When he returned, he sat down for a minute, then got up restlessly, and finally went to the girl's door.

"Hey!"

"Yes?"

"You ever coming out of there?"

"I'll be right out, Mr. Braden."

"Okay." He stood by the door a moment, then called out. "I'll pack my one-suiter. May I leave the rest of the bags here? I'll pick them up when I get back."

"Of course," she answered.

He went to the bedroom and packed the bag. Then he walked back to the living room. The girl entered a moment later. She had changed from skirt and sweater to a cotton house dress, starched and cool-looking. She pushed the ottoman directly in front of his chair, then sat in front of him, fingers interlaced over her knees.

He lifted his glass. "You want a drink?"

She shook her head, spoke up, "If you're going to leave here by seven-thirty, we'd better have dinner now." She started to get up, and he caught her by the hand.

"I'm not hungry."

"Neither am I." Her hand shook slightly in his grasp. He let it go.

"You won't have to drive me up there. I'll call a cab."

"All right."

"I'll call you as soon as I find out anything definite."

"You'll have to call the office if it's before five," she said, then added, irrelevantly, "I start breaking in a new girl tomorrow."

"Don't tell Mario anything until I call you."

"I won't." She looked up at him. "Please be careful of yourself."

"Sure."

She let her head fall forward, resting it on his knee. Braden scowled, gazed across the top of her bent head. He reached out his free hand and laid it softly on the brushed, blond hair.

CHAPTER **9**

THE Hotel Nacionale was cheap, dingy, and at the wrong end of Ensenada. So were most of its patrons. Its sagging façade, embellished with peeling paint and cracked plaster, offered little inducement to the tourist, sports fisherman or seeker of night life. Its bar catered to local boatmen and laborers, and saw an occasional woman on her way to, or from, business with the *norte-americanos*. A forgotten place. That's why Braden chose it.

It offered a place to hide, and a small management to be paid for forgetting he was there. He didn't think anyone in the Baja California town knew him, but he couldn't afford to take any chances. He couldn't allow the Perin woman or Dutch Borg, anyone, to know he was in Ensenada.

He paced the room like a caged animal. It was Tuesday night, and he'd been in the room since sometime after midnight, Sunday. The faded curtains, threadbare rug and musty bedspread were looking worse by the hour. And he hadn't found out a damned thing since leaving Glendale.

Billy Cash had arrived at the car lot at five minutes to eight. He'd jumped from a car, waved a negligent good-by to the girl driving it, and walked over to where Braden and Herndon were standing.

"I'm ready." He was looking at Herndon.

"There it is," Braden said, pointing to the white Mercedes. "You drive that."

"Right." The boy looked at the sports car without interest, then turned back to the football player. "You play good, Pete. I won a bundle last season."

Herndon said he was glad. He didn't look happy about much else. He watched Braden climb into the Oldsmobile. Braden looked through the open car window, bent his head in the direction of Billy Cash. "You follow me to San Diego."

"Follow you? In that?" The boy indicated the Mercedes. "You lost your mind, Braden?"

"You'll follow me if you want the two hundred dollars."

The boy walked to the white car and got in. He started the engine, listened to the uneven cough that would become a screaming whine when the accelerator was near the floor. He waited.

"I'll let you know," Braden said to Herndon.

The athlete nodded, watched as they pulled away.

Three hours later, Braden was talking to the boy outside a tourist cabin at San Ysidro. They'd eaten in San Diego, gassed the two cars, then driven to the small coastal town located in the United States, just north of the Mexican border.

"The Mercedes stays in the car port, Billy. All the time. You take it out, and I come looking for you."

"Okay, okay. What am I supposed to do while you're gone?"

"Stay here. If you get tangled up with a girl, do it here. And don't cross over to Tijuana. Understand?"

"I hear you."

"I should be back sometime Wednesday and I want you here waiting. You have any money?"

"Not a quarter. I lost today. The lousy bucket they hand me to drive, it's a wonder I—"

"Here." Braden pulled two twenties and a ten from his billfold. "Half a bill. Stay sober and be here."

A few minutes later he crossed to Tijuana, then bore left to cut off the main section of the border city. As soon as he was out of the city limits, he let his foot get heavy and began eating up the miles to the seaside town of Ensenada.

Ensenada. He moved to the window, peered down upon the rapidly darkening street. Two lousy days. Now he waited for his landlord. When the knock finally came, he went to the door quickly.

"Who is it?"

"Escamilla, señor."

Braden opened the door. A stocky Mexican entered—Duarte Escamilla, part-time bartender, hotel clerk and procurer. He was a pock-marked man, with intelligent eyes over flaring nostrils and mustaches, the latter worn in the traditional manner. His heavy black hair was carefully parted and combed to one side.

"I sent my woman again," Escamilla offered. He sat rigidly on the straight-backed chair, regarding Braden seriously as he sipped at his brandy.

"Well?" Braden asked impatiently.

"No car, señor. She could see no white car such as you described."

"Damn it!" Braden tossed his drink down, scowling. "She ask anyone?"

"You said not to, Señor Braden."

"Right. How about the two girls?"

"The young women are still at the new hotel by the beach. My woman tells me that one of them has used the pool for swimming, but not the one with the red hair. She understands they will leave for your side tomorrow afternoon." He drank some more of the liquor. "That is all she could learn."

"All right." Braden rose, went to the window again. He spoke without turning. "Tell her to keep quiet about this, Duarte."

"My woman will say only what I tell her to say," the Mexican replied simply.

"Fine. It'll make you some money. You get it when I leave."

"That will be good." Escamilla set his glass on the bureau and left the room.

Braden cursed aloud after the man had gone. Maybe he was down here for a vacation—to see the sights. So far, they'd been limited to a tired hotel room and part of a lazy street. He looked into the almost complete darkness and made up his mind.

Ten minutes later he wandered down a back street. This end of town was dark, not clean. He started across an alley, hesitated, then turned abruptly into the narrow thorough-fare. He moved toward a pale wash of yellow light emanating from the window of an adobe-and-plaster cantina.

El Salon Grande. That's what the sign said in the proper flourishes and geegaws affected by a long-ago sign painter. The blue, gold, and red had faded to almost pastel oblitera-tion. Braden didn't believe it, but he went in anyway.

It was crowded inside. He was the fifth customer and he made it more so. Three men were sitting at a table, one man at the short bar, and a girl was standing before an ancient juke box. There was also a barman. The latter's underwear and apron were visible, the underwear sweat-stained and gray. Braden walked to the bar amid utter si-lence.

The girl held a coin half-in and half-out of the slot, watched his reflection in the glass front of the music maker. The three drinkers at the table looked from under their hats.

"Beer." His voice seemed to thunder in the room.

It came to him warm and in a bottle. No glass. He smiled, turned around and leaned with his elbows on the bar, then looked at the men at the table. He kept looking until the hats tilted forward and the conversation resumed. Then he transferred his gaze to the girl and waited until she pulled the coin clear out of the slot. She read song titles, bent for-ward stiffly and obviously aware of his quiet stare. Braden's smile widened.

The man at the bar cleared his throat, and Braden looked at him. This one was tall and hatless. His black, curly hair was worn too long and framed a quick, handsome face. He moved restlessly, then lifted a finger from the sweating beer bottle held in his hand. The finger pointed in the general direction of the juke box. His voice was soft.

"You think you see something, my friend?" His gaze lay on Braden, as soft as his voice.

"A woman, mister. What better thing to see?" Braden had turned back, was watching the girl again. He could see the young man from the corner of his eye.

The man nodded. "That is true. There is very little better." His eyes narrowed. "You don't like the bars uptown? Or at the big hotels?"

Braden shrugged, played the game. "Who can like or dislike a bar?"

"They are more comfortable for the tourists."

"If one is a tourist." Braden turned back to the bar, pointed at his beer. "Can you fix this?"

The young man laughed and said something in Spanish. The bartender replaced the warm bottle with a cold one. And a glass.

"You have business in Ensenada?" The man moved closer. Both men watched the girl. She had made her choice, dropped the coin.

"I thought I did." They listened to the unleashed trio, watched the girl sway lightly to the mambo beat. When it was over, Braden nodded in her direction. "Yours?"

"For now."

"Do you want to make some money?" Braden asked. The last word hung in new silence, and the man at the bar shifted his position. His eyes were like agates.

"How?" The word was almost whispered.

"Business. Not the kind you think." Braden indicated a vacant table. "Ask her to join us and I'll tell you." He looked at the man. "I don't think you will be talkative if you don't like what I have to say."

"That is true." The man called to the girl in rapid Spanish, then moved with Braden to the table. They waited, standing, until the girl arrived.

"This is Consuela," the young man said. "I am Paco Ruiz."

"Stan Braden."

They shook hands all around and sat down. Braden ordered beers, waiting until they arrived before he spoke. The girl sat close to Ruiz, one hand resting on a white shirt sleeve. She filled a tight red dress, her bare legs reaching into high-heeled shoes. She possessed the usual enormous eyes and clear, olive complexion. She hadn't smiled.

"I came down here on business," he said. "So far, I've been able to do nothing."

"What kind of business?" Ruiz asked.

"I have to find a car."

"A car? There are many—" the Mexican began.

"This is a special car. It's disappeared, and I've got to locate it."

"Why, my friend?"

"Business. That's all I can tell you."

"That ain't enough, mister." It was the girl. She was looking at him, a scowl wrinkling her forehead. "Paco doesn't stick his neck out for anyone unless he knows what's happening."

Braden had turned to her when she started talking, and was now grinning. He held up a hand. "Okay, *pocha*." He looked at Ruiz. "Where in hell did you find her? East Los Angeles?"

"Norwalk." Consuela smiled reluctantly and became almost pretty. "And he didn't find me. I found him."

"She's right, my friend," Ruiz said. "I want no trouble."

"All right," Braden said. He explained about the hotel, the car, and the reason he couldn't look himself. When he'd finished, the man turned to the girl.

"Could you find it if it's in town?" He turned to Braden, explained. "I come from La Paz. Don't know Ensenada."

The girl considered. "I guess so."

"How long would it take you?" Braden asked.

"An hour or so. Who would know where the car is?"

"The girl would know, but we can't ask her. Maybe someone at her hotel," Braden offered.

"How much?" the girl asked.

"Twenty dollars if you locate it. Ten if you don't."

The girl stood up and went to the bar. The bartender handed her a white bag with a carrying strap. She looped it over her shoulder and returned to the table. She said something to Ruiz in Spanish, then turned to Braden. "I'll try it."

She was back in an hour. She came directly to their

table and sat down. "The Mercedes is in a small garage. The man that owns the garage is a mechanic. I understand the car needed some work done on it."

"Who told you that?" Braden asked.

The girl smiled. "No one told me. I learned it from a man. He works at the hotel in the daytime, drinks at a bar when he's off duty. I know where the bar is."

"Do you know where the garage is located?"

"Sure. Near the edge of town. A guy named Tomas Villaron has it."

"Know anything about him?"

"Not much." She shrugged. "I guess he's a good mechanic. I don't think it's a place for foreign cars like a Mercedes. The whole thing smells a little, I think. The car being there."

"You can make book it smells." Braden looked at Ruiz. "Can she take me to this place?"

The young Mexican shook his head. "No. But I can." He spoke with the girl in Spanish, nodded a couple of times, rose from the table. "Come on."

Braden thanked the girl and left with Ruiz.

The two men walked until they'd run out of streets and were almost in the country. The garage lay at the end of a barely discernible lane—a board-and-galvanized-tin-and-tarpaper building. It was ramshackle and leaned toward town. Tiny, weak beams of light shone through its many cracks.

Braden placed a hand on Ruiz' arm and motioned for him to remain behind. He walked undetected to the building, slid along the side. He found a wide crack between two of the vertical boards, and poked a hole in the black paper.

The Mercedes had been placed in a dark corner, two other vehicles between it and the door. He could hardly make it out in the dim illumination provided by the night light. A grease-stained cover had been thrown over the half of the car that faced the door, making it harder to identify. From his vantage point, Braden could see reflections on the white rear deck, could make out the rear license plate. The bracket said "Bel-Air."

He walked back to the small café with Ruiz, not saying much. The car was in Ensenada, and he thought he knew why. Now he could wait.

CHAPTER **10**

THE Mercedes arrived in Tijuana an hour behind Braden and the Oldsmobile. He had already crossed the border and was parked a short distance above the customs building. He could see the International Gate and was settled back in his car, waiting for the action to start. The day after his discovery of the Mercedes in Ensenada, an excited Duarte had come to him early in the day with the news that the girls were packing, getting ready for their return trip to the United States.

Traffic at this place of entry was light on weekday afternoons. Only two customs officers were inspecting the cars as they came through from Mexico. Are you an American citizen? Where were you born, please? Once in a while a look in the turtlebacks. Now and then they made a complete search of a car and luggage. You never knew, so you took your chances.

Braden caught sight of the white car several blocks before it reached the gate. As it neared the check point, a coupe ducked in front of it, arriving at the gate in time to be first. Braden's eyes widened momentarily. He was sure he knew what was coming. And why.

The man driving it acted as though he were nervous. And a little drunk. Braden smiled crookedly, almost heard the conversation. Sure, I'm an American citizen. Born in Nebraska. Yeah, yeah, I had a few drinks in a joint down there. No, I ain't bringing nothing back from Mexico. Trunk? Yeah. Wait'll I find the key.

He got the full treatment. One of the two uniformed men rode to the parking and inspecting area with the nervous man, called another officer from the building to work the gate. The two girls in the white sports car pulled up in the space vacated.

Summer dresses and wind-blown hair. Dark glasses in young faces and, yes, officer, we each bought a leather bag in Mexico. And this serape. The brilliantly colored serape covered the backs of the two bucket seats. Braden grinned cynically and reached for the ignition key. He didn't even look up as the Mercedes passed him.

He lost five minutes at San Ysidro. Billy Cash was waiting and had only to get the white car out of the car port. Braden didn't catch sight of the first white car until he was ten miles north of San Diego, on U.S. Highway 395. He stayed a mile behind, watching the cars that passed him and that passed the Mercedes. Before long a black sedan fell in between his car and the white car. It stayed there. He grunted and settled down to drive.

The girls stopped at a gas station near Camp Elliott, a naval installation, the black sedan pulling ahead two blocks before parking. Braden didn't move when the two cars got under way. He waited. Billy Cash arrived two minutes later, and Braden got out of the Olds. He walked to the other car.

"Okay, Billy."

The boy got out of the white Mercedes and pulled a roll of friction tape from a pocket. He walked to the back of the sedan and quickly altered a three on the license plate, making it a passable eight. He winked at Braden, then took his place behind the wheel of the Olds.

"It's a black Cadillac, kid, '57, I think. Two men in it, about a quarter-mile behind the girls."

"Sedan?"

"Right. Wait until after you make the turn toward Escondido before you make your move. There's a road there that parallels the highway for about six miles. Keep me in your rearview mirror, and when I turn off, you're on your own. You can do it?"

The boy's lip curled. "Are you kidding? Gimme my two bills, Braden. What do I do with this iron when I'm done?"

Braden handed him the money. "Take it back to Herndon and tell him nothing. Go back to the beach and forget it all happened." He waved to the boy, adding, "Don't forget to pull that damned tape off!"

"See you." The boy gunned the Oldsmobile, burning rubber.

Braden, following in the second Mercedes, kept the boy in sight. Fifteen minutes later he made his turn onto the parallel road. He increased his speed and soon was able to see all three cars on the main highway, a half-mile to his left. They were spread out over a mile-and-a-half distance, all traveling at a good rate of speed. He was beginning to wonder if the boy would get his chance in time, when luck entered the picture. He saw the girls begin to slow down, unable to pass a huge truck and trailer, the black sedan doing likewise, but not Billy Cash.

The Oldsmobile could be seen to pick up speed as it closed on the slowing Cadillac. Suddenly it dipped to the right, kissed the black sedan for a fleeting second, then faltered slightly. Almost immediately the Olds was horsed back into the driving lane, then went hurtling down the highway, passing both the girls and the slow-moving highway unit. The black car slewed into the soft shoulder, spewing dust, and came to a twisting halt.

Braden had slowed down when the action started, now was moving slowly along the side road, observing the Cadillac and its occupants. Two men were frenziedly trying to pull a crumpled fender from the left front tire. The half-mile distance was too much for close looking, but it was possible that an axle had been broken. Braden hoped so, then increased his speed and was soon back on the main highway.

The girls didn't stop again until they neared the town of Escondido. Here, they pulled into the parking area of a highway café, a diagonally marked lot, with few cars in evidence. They got out of the car, walked to the front of the restaurant and entered.

Braden arrived a minute behind them. He allowed his car to coast the last fifty yards and come to a halt beside its twin. If the driver of the girl's car hadn't left the keys in it, he'd have to go inside the restaurant and take them away from her. He jumped out, looked at the dashboard of the car they were driving. The keys were still in the ignition lock. No one steals a Mercedes.

He unlocked the trunks of both cars, changed the matched luggage rapidly. The two extra bags and the white coat that were behind the seats of the girl's car he tossed on the seats of the car he'd been driving. He transferred the contents of the four glove compartments, then tossed the serape over the seat backs of his car. He returned both sets of keys to the ignition locks, then changed the registration folders. He stood back and looked at both of the cars. The transfer satisfied him, and he got in the car the girls had arrived in. He parked it behind the restaurant, then went inside via the front door.

She was easy to spot in the nearly empty café. She was sitting in a booth, facing the door, and she looked like her picture. Wind-tossed auburn hair fell to shoulders pressed against the back of the wooden booth. A generous and petulant mouth provided the only coloring in a pallid, strained face—a face marked by high, flat cheekbones. Thin brows arched over large violet eyes. She didn't look as young as her years. The girl with her was blond.

He walked to the booth they were occupying and looked down at the auburn-haired girl.

"Hello, Carol. My name is Braden." He watched her face turn white at the mention of his name. "You know me, huh?"

"What do you want?" she whispered. She looked worn about the eyes. A slight beading of perspiration covered her upper lip.

Braden turned to the other girl. "What's your name, Miss?"

"Peggy Bettner." She turned to Carol, then back to Braden. "Just what is this? Who are—"

"May I sit down? I'm a friend of Carol's father. Right, Carol?"

"Yes." She was staring at Braden, wide-eyed.

The blond girl studied him, hesitated a moment. Her eyes reflected puzzlement and a little doubt.

"If you're a friend of Carol's, and have good sense, you'll listen to what I have to say," Braden said quietly.

The girl looked at Carol quickly, then looked up at Braden. She nodded her head, and he slipped into the booth, next to Carol Ashe.

"All right. You've got some sense. Now, we're in a hurry. I'll explain why, later. Right now I'd like to have you answer a couple of questions. Will you?" he asked.

The girl licked her lips nervously. "What are they?"

"Did Carol go swimming at Ensenada?"

"No, but that could be—"

"It could, but probably wasn't," he broke in. "Did she seem nervous to you?"

"Well, I . . ." She looked at the auburn-haired girl again, bit her lip. "I don't see where you—"

"Please answer it, Peggy," Braden said.

"Yes, she was nervous. She didn't have a good time down there," Peggy Bettner said hurriedly.

"Okay." Braden looked across the table, said seriously, "If you want to help Carol you'll do as I suggest. When I'm through talking, you can ask her if I'm right."

Peggy Bettner looked him in the eye. "I won't even talk to you if I don't know who you are."

"I told you. My name is Braden. Stan Braden. I'm a friend of Clayton Ashe."

"Is that right, Carol?" The girl didn't take her eyes off Braden.

"That's his name," Carol said in a dead voice.

"All right, Mr. Braden. Go ahead," the girl said.

"Carol is in a jam. She doesn't know how big it is herself, and I'm not entirely sure. But it's a jam. And you could be involved. Right up to your neck." He heard the intake of breath from the girl by his side and turned to her. "You didn't know that, did you, Carol?" He turned back to Peggy. "Here's what you've got to do, Peggy. Drive that car back to Los Angeles. Fast, and alone. Are you living at the sorority house during the summer?"

The girl nodded.

"When you get back to Los Angeles, park the car near the police station on First Street. Then take a cab to the campus. I understand you're on a flight to New York tomorrow morning."

Her eyes widened. "Yes, I am. How did you—"

"Never mind. Take the flight and forget about this. Don't mention it to anyone. Not anyone. When it's all over, Carol may want to tell you about it. That's up to her."

The girl looked at Carol. "What should I do?"

The auburn-haired girl looked harassed. She cupped her face in her hands and shook her head. Finally, she looked up. "You'd better do as he says, Peggy."

"Are you sure? If you—"

"I'm sure." Carol's shoulders slumped. "I shouldn't have asked you to come." She looked up. "Someday I may tell you why. He's right. You'd better drive back alone," she said harshly.

Peggy Bettner looked at the girl a moment, then let her eyes rest on Braden. "You'll take care of her?"

He nodded.

"You'd better. I know your name." The college girl was fighting tears and fright, not fully understanding any of it. She rose, took a last look at Carol. "Be careful, honey."

Braden had risen, put out a hand. "You're a hell of a girl, Peggy."

The girl looked at his hand, hesitated, then accepted it. "Just remember, Mr. Braden. You'd better take care of her."

"I will." He started for the entrance with her. "Do those two bags and white coat belong to you?"

"Yes." They stood at the door.

"When you get in that car, keep going. Don't stop for anything, and don't let anything pass you. Can you floorboard it if you have to?"

"I can corner it, Mr. Braden. I've road-raced my brother's Jag."

"Good. Lotsa luck, kid." He watched her roar from the parking lot, listening to the engine as it quickly reached a snarling whine. He was about to rejoin Carol when he stopped suddenly. A Yellow Cab sped by the restaurant, two passengers in the rear seat. They were leaning forward, one pointing to the rapidly diminishing sports car. Braden half-smiled. They wouldn't catch the blond girl. Not in a cab, they wouldn't.

He returned to the booth, called for the check and paid it, then reached down for Carol Ashe. "Come on." He led her from the restaurant, around to the back. She put a hand to her mouth when she saw the second white car.

"Why, that's—"

"Yeah. Get in."

She climbed in without a word and sank back in her seat.

He headed in the same direction as Peggy Bettner and the Yellow Cab, keeping miles behind them both. Twenty minutes later he turned from the main highway at Rainbow. He dropped down a secondary road to the town of Fallbrook. He pulled up and parked just before they entered the city limits.

"All right, Carol." He glanced down at her lap. She was nervously shredding a small handkerchief. "Why did Samson want you to go to Ensenada?"

"I delivered a package of money to a man at the hotel," she said sullenly.

"How about your car in that Mexican garage?"

"Samson told me to do that, too."

"Why did you have to invite Peggy?"

"He said it would look more natural if two girls were together," she said. ˍ

"Yeah." Braden lit a cigarette, then looked at her. There was a shiny film of perspiration on her forehead. "You know what we're going to do now?"

She didn't answer.

"We're going to a motel. As man and wife. If you have any objections, I'll drive you to Santa Barbara. Now." He waited. "No objections?"

She shook her head.

They found a place with enclosed garages instead of the

usual open car port. It lay at the edge of the prosperous little community. She sat in the car while he registered, made no comment until he'd closed the door behind them in the cabin.

"What about my luggage?"

"On the way to L.A. It'll take 'em a long time to figure out the car isn't yours. If they find out at all." He glanced at her. "Oh, yeah. Your car is in the garage. Peggy drove a duplicate to Los Angeles." He eyed the cabin. One large bedroom, a bath and a small kitchen; twin beds and one closet. He'd asked for a unit as far from the street as possible where it would be quiet. The court owner had obliged, and they were in the deepest cabin on the property.

The girl started for the bathroom, and he got between her and the door.

"Give me your bag."

"What?" Her eyes narrowed.

"I said give me your bag."

She stared at him angrily, then handed it over. He opened it and searched it thoroughly. All he found was a small teaspoon. He tossed spoon and purse on one of the beds.

"All right, Carol, where's the rest of it?"

She didn't answer him, started for the front door. He grabbed her by the arm, swung her to face him. "Take off your sweater."

"You go to hell, Braden," she said furiously. "Who do you—"

He slapped her face—hard. Tears sprang to her eyes, and she covered her face with both hands. He pulled her hands away roughly. "Take off the sweater."

She complied, tearing two buttons from the cardigan in the process. She threw it at him. He felt the pockets, the hem, then tossed it next to the purse.

"The dress."

"Are you crazy?" she began, but started unbuttoning the front of the dress as he advanced toward her. He waited. She stepped out of the garment, kicked it toward him. He went through it, tossed it aside. She wore no slip, only two white pieces of clothing, plus saddle shoes and socks.

"You ready to give it up?"

"I don't know what you—" she began.

"Take off your brassière."

Her face blanched.

"Take it off or I'll rip it off," he said flatly. "Or you can scream."

She reached between full breasts, pulled out a package and threw it at him. He picked up the small, cellophane-covered bundle and moved to the girl's side. He grasped her by the arm.

"You wanted to visit the bathroom? Come on. You can watch." He pulled the shrinking girl to the door, opened it and forced her into the bathroom with him. She began pummeling him with her fists. He leaned against her heavily, said, "Don't get carried away, tramp. This is just the beginning."

She watched him with dead eyes as he opened the package. She was jammed into a corner, arms against her body, his back and side holding her in that position. She was helpless to move. He unwrapped the cellophane package and let the contents lie in the palm of one hand. An eyedropper, a tiny and shining needle, and five capsules. Only the spoon was missing, and he'd found that in her purse. The girl began to whimper as he reached for the toilet tissue.

He smashed the eyedropper in folds of tissue, flushed it, the needle, and the capsules down the toilet. Then hauled the girl to the closest bed and pulled back the covers. "Take off your shoes and socks," he ordered.

She sat on the edge of the bed and did as he asked.

"Get under the covers."

The girl obeyed, pulled the covers up to her shoulders. He reached out a hand.

"The rest."

She turned her face to the wall, away from him. She reached her arms up her back, unhooked the brassière and handed it to him. Then slipped her pants off and kicked them out the side of the bed. She put her hands behind her head and raised herself on the pillow, deliberately allowing the movement to bare her to the waist. Her lip curled.

"You'd better hurry. Before I get too sick." She looked down at her breasts with disgust. "I'm for free, Braden. Is there anything special you have in mind?"

Braden picked up the underwear from the floor and walked close to the bed. He reached out a hand, and the girl tightened her lips, didn't move. He took hold of the covers and pulled them over her. "How much stuff you using?"

"A spoon a day," she whispered.

He whistled soundlessly. "When did you fix last?"

"At the service-station rest room. Near Camp Elliott."

"A regular jolt?"

"No. Light. I didn't want Peggy to notice anything. I've been half-sick for two days."

He nodded. "You should start getting good and sick in about two more hours. Right?"

She turned her face to the wall again. "I guess so."

"If I call a doctor, he'll see that you get a fix. He'll also call the police. I can't afford that and neither can you. We can kick it here. Cold. What do you want to do?"

"It doesn't matter," she mumbled. "I'm finished anyway."

"Maybe not," Braden said, picking up her dress, shoes, socks and sweater. "This guy Samson has you over a barrel, huh?"

She nodded, turned to face him.

"Maybe I have him over one now." He started for the door.

The girl spoke up. "Why are you taking my clothes? I won't leave."

Braden opened the door, then looked back. "Not unless you want to leave naked, you won't."

CHAPTER 11

IT WASN'T hard to find. In the darkened garage he'd gone over the Mercedes with a flashlight—the trunk, interior, and engine. Underneath the sports car he'd reached up to the darkest recesses of the running gear, and there it was. A black, oilcloth package, wired so securely it took him minutes with pliers to remove it.

He unwrapped the oilcloth on the seat of the car, and four smaller bundles were exposed. Using the flashlight for illumination, he carefully cut through the plastic covering of one bundle. Under the plastic were even smaller packets. He opened one.

Heroin. Probably as pure as could be brought from the south side of the line. He estimated the amount. It was plenty big, even for narcotics. Two kilos, altogether. Four and two-fifths pounds. He calculated rapidly. From kilos into pounds into ounces. After that, spoons and half-spoons. Then into capsules. Caps. Through many hands and many cuts in strength. Each hand taking more and more money for each dwindling unit of the cut heroin. The girl probably delivered eighteen to twenty thousand dollars in cash for the narcotics. In capsules, and cut many times, it represented a quarter of a million dollars. And many lifetimes of misery. He hated to touch the stuff.

He stared at the innocent-looking bundles for another moment, then carefully rewrapped them and left them on the seat of the car. He opened the garage doors, backed the car out into the sunlight and drove away.

He parked in the business section of the small town and carried the heroin into a liquor store. He made his purchases and asked for a small cardboard carton, wrapping paper and string. He placed the sausage-shaped bundles in the carton, stuffed newspaper around them until they fit snugly, then wrapped and tied the carton, and addressed the package to himself at San Fernando, California.

From the liquor store he went to a drugstore, bought a four-cent envelope and addressed it to Jean Webster. He asked directions to the local Greyhound depot. There he checked the package through to San Fernando via Greyhound Express. He asked that the package be held at San Fernando until he presented the claim check. He dropped the check into the envelope and posted it.

Back at the drugstore he entered a public phone booth. He looked at his watch, saw it was nearly 6:30 P.M. He placed a call to the Citrus number, collect. He heard Jean Webster say she'd accept the charges.

"Hello?"

"Hi, kid."

"Mr. Braden!" There was a short silence, then: "I've been wondering if you'd— Is everything all right?"

"Everything is all right. I'll settle with you for this call when I get back to L.A. Okay?"

"Of course," she replied quickly, then asked: "Did you find the girl?"

"I found her."

"Oh." A slight pause. "Are you going to take her to Santa Barbara and—"

"Not yet," he broke in. "I can't for a while. It'll be a week or more before I can come in to L.A. You'll find out why when I get there. In the meantime, will you do something for me? A couple of things?"

"Yes. What are they?"

"First, call Pete Herndon and tell him the girl is with me and is all right." He winced at this one. "Tell him to report his Mercedes stolen. You understand? *His* car."

"Yes, I'll tell him."

"Good. Is Mario back yet?"

"Not yet." There was another pause. "Your suit came back from the cleaners. The bloodstains came out."

"Yeah? Well, thanks for—"

"You will be careful . . . Stan?"

"Sure. Here's the other thing you can do for me. You'll get a letter in a couple of days. From Fallbrook. When you get it, take it to the office and put it in the safe. Mario has one, hasn't he?"

"Yes."

"Well, put it there. Don't keep the letter around the house. I'll ask you for it when I need it. Don't even tell Mario about it if he comes back."

"I'll take care of that."

"Thanks. And, kid . . ." He hesitated, shook his head. "Never mind. I'll see you." He hung up, looked at the telephone for a moment, then put in a call to Ashe.

"Clay?"

"Stanley? Where in the world have—"

"Never mind," he interrupted. "I haven't time to go into any of it. I have Carol."

There was a long silence, then the older man asked quietly, "How is she?"

"I can't . . . Now wait a second and listen . . . Listen. I've got her, but I can't bring her home yet."

"Why not? Is there anything—"

"If you'll shut up a minute, I'll tell you." He waited. "Now, can I talk?"

"Of course, Stanley. Go ahead."

"There's a reason I can't bring her home now. A good reason, but I can't tell it to you. She may, later. She'll be all right, and I'll take good care of her. She'll be with me all the time."

"How long?"

"Couple of weeks, maybe. Maybe less." There was a pause, then Ashe's voice came through.

"Very well," he said. "I'll trust to your judgment."

"Good. I'll call you later. Or have Carol call you. And for Christ's sake, stop worrying so much." Braden replaced the receiver and left the booth.

He bought a handful of pocket-sized books in the drugstore, then went to a near-by grocery. He purchased two boxes of soft candy bars, twenty-four to a box; four quarts of milk, several cellophane-covered cakes and pies, bacon, eggs, bread, coffee and sugar, canned soup and canned beans, butter and cigarettes.

Back at the auto court he stopped by the manager's cabin and sounded his horn. An elderly man came out, leaned over the car door.

"Yes, Mr. Williams?"

Braden smiled. "Just thought I'd tell you we'll be sticking pretty close to our cabin. My wife's had some nervous trouble lately." He grinned with sudden candor. "That's why I asked for twin beds. I decided to give her a week of absolute quiet. She didn't want to go to a nursing home or a hospital, so we picked Fallbrook. Nice, quiet little town."

The manager smiled. "Sure is, Mr. Williams. You people just take it easy back there. Won't nobody bother you and won't be no noise, neither. Anything I can do, just call me."

Braden thanked the man and drove back to the unit. He put the car away, closed and locked the garage doors. Inside, he stored the provisions, then sat down in an occasional chair and waited. It began about nine o'clock that night.

She had the covers pulled closely about her and was perspiring profusely. Dull eyes no longer roamed the room, but bored silently into the wall. The auburn head moved from side to side, and she began to make the sounds accompanying nausea. Getting ready to be sick, she clutched the bedspread to her and slipped out of bed.

In the bathroom he held her head, let her slump against him as heaving convulsions wracked her body. When the attack was over, she staggered back to the bed, bedspread trailing. He saw the tracks—the marks left by the needle. They were mostly dark and on her left upper arm. Some were still red and welted. No wonder she wouldn't go swimming in Ensenada. He saw the young body, firm flesh over good bones, a general pallidness the only sign of her addiction. She noticed him staring at her and looked down at her own nakedness.

"What's the matter, Braden? My seams crooked or something?" She flopped on the bed and curled up.

"How long a run?" he asked.

"Six months," she replied dully.

"How'd you stay in such good shape?"

"Never had to kick the habit before," she gasped. "No withdrawal pains because I always had enough to stay in good shape. Real fancy shape." Her teeth began to chatter, and she hugged the pain to herself and left him for the blessed semicoma that keeps an addict from going insane.

He hung his coat in the closet and kicked off his shoes. He picked up one of the books he'd bought. He believed her. It was the tearing results of the withdrawal pains that showed so markedly on addicts, not the actual use of the narcotic itself. If she'd had a steady supply, she wouldn't have had that problem. He started to read, settled into a Western.

"Braden!"

It was almost a scream. She was sitting up straight, arms crossed over her breasts, fingers digging into her shoulders. He got up from the chair, moved to the bed.

"What is it?"

"I'm awfully sick." She let her head fall forward.

"You want to kick, don't you?"

"Yes," she said, starting to cry. "But I can't do it, Braden. I need a fix. Bad." She let herself fall to one side, wiped her wet mouth on the dirtied bedspread.

He looked down at her, went back to the chair. Before he opened the book he looked over at her, said quietly:

"You're *going* to do it, baby."

Later that night he went into the small kitchen and opened a bottle of the whiskey he'd bought. He made a highball. He got back in the bedroom in time to help the girl to the bathroom. She didn't quite make it. Two hours later he was bending over her, massaging cramped legs with rubbing alcohol. She regarded him unseeingly, lips white against the hurt.

For the next three days and nights he let her out of his

sight only once. She promptly tried to hang herself from the shower-curtain bar with two towels, tied together. After that, everywhere she went, he went.

When it got too bad, he poured whiskey down her by the glassful. It made her sick but seemed to take away some of the agony. He finally had to carry her to the bathroom. Something hidden beneath the hurt, filth, and degradation finally rebelled at this invasion of privacy, and she clawed at his face.

Braden slept only when the girl fell into short periods of immobility. Even then, he was aware of every move she made; every pain-ridden, convulsive jerk of her body. He would snap awake, leave his bed and automatically cover the writhing girl with the sheet. She would just as automatically throw it off, anxious to free crawling skin.

Those first three days she talked little, mostly crying or moaning softly when it became unbearable. She burrowed her face deeply in the sodden pillow, not looking at him.

The room smelled like a pigsty.

He spent most of his time in the chair watching her and helping when he could. Near dawn of the fourth day the first streaks of light reflected on four empty whiskey bottles. Most of it had gone into her and out of her, counteracting and numbing. Now she was in the first few minutes of actual sleep. He knew what would happen when she awakened, and he waited for it, waited for the hard part.

After a while she stirred, then sat up slowly. She pulled the sheet about her upper body and looked around at the filthy bed, the room, Braden. She raised a hand to her matted hair.

"My God! What a mess!" She covered her face with her hands.

"Yeah."

"Why did you do it?" She peered at him from terrible eyes.

He shrugged. "I did it, and you're almost through. You may make it all the way."

She shut her eyes and leaned back. "All right. The tab

comes later, I suppose. Who pays it? My father?" She looked at him.

"Maybe. He wants you to come home."

"He told me."

"That was months ago. He's asking again."

"I'm answering again. No."

Braden stood up and gazed at the girl for a moment. He put his hands in his pockets and looked her over slowly. She bit her lower lip, stared back defiantly.

"Okay, tramp." An indrawn breath was the only sign she'd heard him. Her knuckles showed white. "I had to tell you what your father wants because he asked me to. I'm glad you answered the way you did. Clay's better off without you. Besides, you're right. Look at what he did to you: after you did him the favor of living in the comfortable home he provided for you and your mother, wore the clothes he bought, ate the food he earned, he repaid you by being a lousy ex-convict. You should have left long ago. A crumby old—"

"Shut up!" the girl said wildly.

"—a crumby old man with a record isn't the sort of father to show your friends," Braden went on. "You must have been real ashamed to—"

"I couldn't help it, Braden!" she cried out, pushed her face into the pillow. "I just couldn't help it," she said, muffled. She began to sob.

He didn't answer. He stepped to the bed, lifted the weeping girl out of the sheet and carried her to the bathroom. He reached for the shower faucets with one hand, holding the weak girl upright with the other. When the water assumed a tepid flow, he shoved her under it.

"Stay in there until I come after you."

Back in the bedroom he stripped the linen from her bed. He made a bundle of it in the bedspread and placed it by the door. Then went back to the bathroom.

The girl was on the floor of the stall shower. Her back jammed into the corner, her head between her knees. She'd made an attempt at washing her hair.

Braden took off his shirt and T-shirt, then reached in and grabbed her by the shoulders. He pulled her close enough to lean against him. From a position on his knees, he finished washing her hair. And the rest of her. He dried her off, then wrapped her in one of the blankets. She stared at him, absolute hate in her eyes.

"You dirty bastard!" she said distinctly. "You dirty, cold-blooded bastard!"

"Sure." He picked her up and laid her on the bed, then got her clothes. He gathered the linen from the floor. "I'll be back soon. If you leave that bed while I'm gone, I'll slap you silly."

He left the court and drove to town. He asked directions to a laundermat, found it, and washed the linen and bedspread. He had them dried, then hurried back to the cabin. The girl was still on the bed, under the blanket. He sat her in the chair, blanket and all, and made up the bed. He put her in it, then went to the kitchen. He came back with a box of twenty-four candy bars, soft and sweet.

"You're hungry," he said.

"Yes." Her eyes burned a hole in the box.

She ate seven of them, fell into troubled sleep for an hour. She awakened then, and ate four more. He fixed her some warm milk and she drank it thirstily. She lost that. He gave her back her underwear, and she put it on under the covers. The day wore on and she ate and slept, gradually retaining more and more of the food. Cake, pie, and candy, anything sweet. It was late afternoon when the first one hit her—tearingly.

The first yen, the all-encompassing desire for more narcotics that comes after the first harsh withdrawal pains have gone. Transcending everything else in the world, it makes everything else seem unimportant.

He'd been waiting for it to happen; knew it was inevitable. He couldn't feel complete empathy for this girl; couldn't realize all that was happening to her, but he could recognize it. He'd seen it before.

She begged him, piteously, for any kind of drug that

would ease the frantic desire. She told him the names of things he could buy over a drugstore counter without a prescription. She got to her knees and embraced his legs. She groveled and cried, then cursed him, gutter language coming easily to her lips.

With only one thing to offer him, she offered that. She stripped off the brassière, then the pants. Eyes bright, she spent minutes telling him what she'd do for him, carefully and specifically, thinking up new things as she talked. She postured and degraded herself. He laughed at her, and she threw herself on her bed, cursing him again.

Exhausted, she finally slept. Then woke up and ate more candy, drank more warm milk. She couldn't stop eating. In between, she ranted at him and talked wildly. She tried to get away, and he wouldn't let her go. When he had to leave the room, he tied her to the bed and left her that way while he lay in the bed beside her, getting needed sleep.

On the sixth day it was over. All of it. She woke stronger and hungrier. She wanted real food. He gave her all her clothes, and she dressed carefully, then fixed her face and her hair. He suggested that she cook breakfast, and she cooked a huge one. She avoided his eyes as they ate, and over coffee he asked her, directly and quietly:

"What happened to you, Carol? I want all of it."

She flushed.

"We've got to talk about it," he said. "I'm taking you back this afternoon." He saw the fear in her face. "Whatever it is, I don't think Samson will move before he talks with me. I can damned near guarantee it."

Carol Ashe shook her head. "The way you've seen me these last few—"

"Forget that," he broke in. "Or remember it if you want. Maybe it'll give you something to think about if you start looking for a needle. But don't worry about it. You weren't a woman as far as I was concerned. You were a damned dope addict. That makes you nothing. Neither man nor woman. Nothing." He looked at her bent head. "Tell it, Carol."

"All right." She looked up, her eyes full of tears. "First, I want to tell you about my father. I was terribly wrong, Braden. Terribly wrong. Only trouble was, when I realized it, it was too late." She drank some coffee. "At first, I was bitter. I thought he'd ruined my life. I haven't any excuse," she said, raising her eyes again, "except that I acted like a child instead of an adult. The only thing I want to do now is be in a position to go home and ask him to forgive me."

"You may be able to, and real soon." Braden rose, re-filled their cups. He leaned over, punched the girl lightly on the chin. "I take back the tramp, Carol." He smiled briefly, settled back in his chair. "Now. Let's have it."

"I don't know exactly," she said, tears again threatening to spill out of the violet eyes. "I just don't know for sure. I had an apartment in North Hollywood, and this girl and I got pretty friendly—I met her on a party somewhere—so I moved in with her. We were—"

"I know all about Lila," he broke in. "How come she didn't know what house in Palos Verdes belonged to Perin?"

"When we were on that party out there, Grace Perin was on a buying trip in the east," the girl explained. "Besides, Lila was so looped she wouldn't have noticed whose house she was in."

"Okay. I know about Lila. Also about the pills, the sorority, the school and the marijuana. How about the heavy stuff?"

She put both hands to her temples and began again. "After I left Lila's I began to drift around from place to place. I started waking up most of the time at Grace's . . ." She trailed off.

"The heroin," Braden said patiently. "The Perin woman is a user, isn't she?"

"How did you—"

"The first time I saw her in the dress shop I suspected something was different about her. I couldn't put my finger on it then. Later on, I figured out that she was at least sniffing coke."

Carol Ashe nodded. "At home she uses heroin. She only uses cocaine at the shop." She paused for a moment. "Anyway, it started easy. Real easy. A couple of pops with Grace —to keep her company—then one every morning to get up on. Just in the skin. Nothing main-line." Her face twisted suddenly. "See, Braden, I know all the words."

"Stan," he said. "Go on."

"I got hooked, that's all. In a few weeks I had to have it or get sick. She let me get sick one morning. Not very sick. Just enough to show me how bad it could get. Then, she fixed me," she said bitterly.

"Main-line?"

She nodded.

"What next?"

"Months of it. Until I was fixing four times a day. There wasn't anything else in the world. I ran out of money and was afraid to ask my father for more. He would have given it to me, but I was afraid he'd find out about the heroin and try to stop me." She picked up her cup. "I didn't have to worry about money, though," she added. "They kept me supplied." She looked over the rim of her cup. "Where did you get the marks on your face, Braden? Did Pete Herndon do it?"

"You know better than that. The two happiness boys you sent did it."

"The two happi—" She stopped, puzzled. "I didn't send anyone to hurt you. The only person I called was Pete."

"You didn't call me?"

"No. Never."

"Someone did. A woman." He shrugged. "I'll probably find out who it was when I contact Samson." He looked over at her. "What does he have on you?"

She looked down at her cup, shook her head.

"Tell me, God-damn it!" he said angrily. "How in hell can I help you if I'm in the dark?"

"Pictures," she said, not looking up. "Moving pictures."

"What kind?"

"Pornographic," she whispered, face flaming. "I hate to tell you this, Brade—Stan."

"How'd he get 'em?" he asked calmly.

"They let me get sick again, then gave me a big fix. I was as high as a person can get." She paused.

"Well?"

"They took my clothes off," she said. "All of them. At the time I thought it was a good idea."

"Who did it?"

"Grace Perin, Samson, and a man I hadn't seen before. A girl, too. A blond girl. I'm sure the man was a user."

"Why?"

"Because he didn't do anything to me. Just touched me." She looked at him levelly, eyes stark. "I can't believe I'm telling anyone this."

"It's a pretty good cleanser, kid. What happened next?"

"Samson. He came over one day when I was fixed and coasting and ran the film for me." She shuddered. "That's it. He suggested I stay at Grace's permanently. Then he suggested this trip. He offered to run the movies for my father if I didn't approve of his suggestions." Her face tightened. "I think I'd kill myself if my father ever saw that film."

Braden was silent for a moment, then reached out a hand and placed it over one of her tightly clenched fists.

"All right, Carol. Maybe I can get you off the hook. Maybe. Can you stay clean?"

"I hope so," she said. "Jesus Christ, but I hope so!"

"You may have to get some help."

"I'll get it," she said fervently, looked at him with a puzzled expression. "How do you know so much about narcotics, Stan? Did you have a habit once?"

"Jails," he said shortly. "I've been in a few. Held seventy-two hours for investigation several times, then kicked out. Some jails have special tanks for addicts, others haven't. I've nursed a few while they were kicking their habits in jails that have no special quarters for narcotic users. I've gone through the whole bit several times." He looked at her. "I met your father in prison. Fifteen years ago."

"Oh." Her eyes widened. "Is that why you helped me?"

"One of the reasons. Not all of it, though. Clay's paying me wages. Good wages. I wouldn't have done it for nothing," he said candidly.

She nodded. "What are we going to do now?"

"We're leaving for L.A. about five this evening," he said, getting up. "You'd better take it easy for the rest of the day." He walked to the bedroom door. "Oh, yeah. If you come out of this okay, you can thank that football player you called. Without his help it would have been a lot tougher for me."

"Pete," she breathed.

"Yeah. He thinks about you."

Her eyes filled with tears again, and she shook her head. "I hope I have the courage to make it."

"Make it?" Braden remained in the doorway a moment, one arm braced against the frame. "Listen. When you kicked that habit cold, you did something it takes a damned good man to do. Besides that, you just finished telling me a story. Not many people could have told it." He looked at her with a twisted grin. "Honey, you may have invented guts."

CHAPTER **12**

IT WAS nearly seven o'clock in the evening when he turned into the quiet street in Atwater. He let the white car roll silently into the driveway and turned off the ignition. They had used the back roads and secondary highways all the way to Los Angeles. No freeways, no main arteries. He glanced at the house; the lights were on.

"Let's go," he said.

The Webster girl's eyes widened when she opened the back door. She looked at Braden and Carol Ashe, then opened the door wider.

"Come in." She led the way into the front room. She smiled at Carol when introduced, pointed out the big chair to Braden, then seated herself on the divan, next to Carol. She looked at Braden expectantly.

"I need your help again, kid," he said. "For a couple of days."

"What do you want me to do, Mr. Braden?"

"I have to be sure Carol is somewhere safe. Where no one can locate her." He lit a cigarette, scowling. "I know damned well I'm imposing on you, but this is important." He looked up. "Before I explain it, can you fix Carol up with some clothes? Her stuff may be gone for good, and she's been in those clothes for a week."

"Of course." Jean rose. "Come with me, Carol. We'll get you fixed up right now." She looked the Ashe girl over. "I think my clothes will fit you. Maybe a little loose in spots, but we'll make something work." She smiled, and the girls left the room.

Jean was back in five minutes and resumed her seat. She told Braden the other girl was taking a shower.

"Now, what is it?" she asked.

He leaned forward. "This girl has had a bad time. Real bad. Maybe she'll tell you about it. Anyway, I have to keep her out of sight for two or three days. And she can't be left alone."

"Why not?"

"I'd rather have her tell you," he said, then asked: "Has Mario returned yet?"

"No. He wired he'll be gone another week, anyway."

"Good. Is there any way you can stay away from the office? Stay home?"

"Well, I don't know about that." She frowned.

"How about the girl you've been breaking in?"

"I'm not sure whether Mr. D'Angelo would . . ." She trailed off uncertainly, then made up her mind. "I suppose she could handle the office all right for a couple of days. I can phone her tonight and meet her with the keys in the morning." She looked at Braden. "This will only take two or three days?"

"I'm sure of it," he said. "One thing: when you take her the keys, make sure Carol goes with you."

"I will." She rose. "May I fix you a drink? Or some coffee?"

"No thanks, kid." He stood, walked to the bathroom door and knocked. "Can you hear me, Carol?"

"Yes, Stan."

"I have to leave," he called out. "You're going to stay here for a couple of days."

Carol Ashe opened the door and stepped into the hallway. She wore a chenille robe and had a towel wrapped around her head.

"It's all right with her?" she asked.

"Yes. Remember what I told you. No calls to anyone, and don't leave the house by yourself."

"I'll remember." She grasped the lapels of his jacket and let her head fall to his chest. "Please straighten it out, Stan."

"Sure." He pushed her away gently. "It shouldn't take long."

"All right." She moved toward Jean's bedroom door, then turned. "Thanks," she said quietly.

He went into the other bedroom, picked up his bags, then noticed his suit hanging on the back of the closet door. It was still in the cleaner's bag. He hooked one finger through the curved hanger handle and started for the back door. Jean Webster met him in the dining room and he nodded toward the covered suit.

"What do I owe you for this?"

She smiled. "I don't know. They brought it along with some of my cleaning and the ticket is still on the bag." She indicated a pink ticket pinned to the bag. "It's made out to me, but your suit is on the list somewhere."

"Is it okay if I settle with you later? For the suit and that long-distance call? Right now, I'm sort of in a—"

"Of course." She walked the rest of the way to the door with him. "What are you going to do now?"

"Take the car back to Herndon's. I don't want anything around here that might lead anyone to Carol. Did you put that envelope in the office safe?"

"Yes."

"Just leave it there until I ask for it."

She nodded, then asked: "Will the rest of this be dangerous?"

"I don't think so." He hesitated, reached for the doorknob. "You don't have to do all this, you know. If you—"

"It's all right," she assured him. "I get lonesome here. I'll enjoy having company." She paused, and the color rose in her cheeks. "Again."

He half-smiled. "See you." He carried the bags to the car, tossed them in, then drove to Glendale. He parked on a side street and walked a block to the car lot. The towheaded man saw him coming and met him halfway on the graveled surface.

"Where is she?"

Braden shook his head. "We have to talk first, Herndon." He nodded at one of the cars. "Can we sit in that one?"

The football player didn't answer, walked to the sedan and opened both doors. He climbed in the rear. Braden slid under the wheel to the far side of the front seat, turned and leaned his arms on the back.

"Before I tell you, I have to know a few things. You ready?"

Herndon studied him a moment, then leaned back. "Go ahead."

"You go for this girl, huh?"

"I already told—"

"I know what you told me," Braden broke in. "Right now I want to hear more. I know what the girl thinks of you. Or I can guess, anyway. What I want to know is how you feel about her."

"Okay, Braden," Herndon admitted. "She's for me."

"Enough to hear something rough?"

"Why, yeah. . . . Yeah, I guess so. What is it?" Herndon leaned forward.

"Narcotics, for one thing." Braden watched the athlete. "You knew about that?"

"I had it figured."

"You were right. She's been doing it for too long and has had a heavy habit. But there's more."

"How bad?"

"Bad enough. You sure as hell won't like it."

"What?" Herndon was scowling.

"Pictures," Braden said flatly. "Motion pictures."

Herndon's lips tightened. "Dirty?"

"No," Braden lied. "Not dirty. Just no clothes."

"Who did it, Braden?" The football player's eyes were cold, his voice low. "Who got that kid on dope?"

Braden shook his head. "It doesn't matter now. What matters is that I work it out and get the film back."

"Where is she?"

"Jean Webster's. Until I can deliver her to her father."

"I still don't see how a girl like that could get started on—"

"It's easy," Braden broke in harshly. "Easy. She really started the day she found out about her old man. You know about that, huh? Anyway, that, and the way things were at school, tripped her up. Guess she felt as though she'd been rejected by the whole damned world. After that all she needed was someone to push her a little. That someone was around." He lit a cigarette, continued. "Before she found out she'd been a fool, it was too late." He exhaled a cloud of smoke. "It happens every day. Businessmen, professional men, thieves, whores, shopgirls, schoolgirls. Even athletes."

Herndon nodded. "What can I do?"

"Nothing right now, except loan me another car."

"Another? Where's the Mercedes I let you have?"

"Somewhere in Los Angeles. Downtown. Did you report it stolen?"

"Yes. Soon as I heard from Jean Webster."

"Good. It should have been picked up by the police by now. You should hear about it any day now."

"What about Carol's car?"

"Her car is a block away from here. When I leave, follow

me and pick it up. I want it out of sight. I'll explain the reasons later."

"Okay."

"Now, do I get another car?" Braden asked.

"Come on." Herndon got out of the car, led the way to the back of the lot. "I can let you have a Ford."

"Good. I'll switch my bags from the Mercedes. Did the kid return the Olds?"

"Wednesday night. What happened to the fender? He wouldn't tell me a thing."

"He wouldn't. It's quite a story, but I haven't time to tell it to you now."

"I'll wait," Herndon said, then asked: "You say Carol is staying with Jean Webster?"

"Yeah."

"Where in hell did *you* ever come up with a girl like her?"

"She's my attorney's secretary," Braden said shortly. "That's all."

Herndon opened the door of a late model Ford sedan. He let Braden slide in.

"How long will it take?" Herndon asked. He leaned on the door sill.

"Couple of days, anyway." Braden started the engine, then turned to the athlete. "Don't even think about going near Jean's house, or phoning, until I say so. Now, follow a couple of minutes behind me and pick up Carol's car."

"Okay." Herndon stepped back from the car. "Luck, Braden."

Palos Verdes lay quietly under clear night skies and a quarter moon, the calm Pacific black and glinting beneath the stars. Braden let the car come to a stop, looked at his watch before he alighted. 10:00 P.M. He looked up and saw the three posing cocks metallically outlined above the garage gables. He started for the door and almost made it. It opened just before he got there. Grace Perin looked at him stonily.

"You must be insane, Braden."

"I want to see Samson."

"He wants to see you." Her lips thinned, and she stood back from the door. "Come in."

She led him through a foyer, past a sunken living room, then down a short hallway. The solid door at the end opened to a patio and pool. Simulated hurricane lamps electrically illuminated the area.

Two men and a woman were seated at the pool's edge. One of the men was Dutch Borg. He jumped to his feet as Braden came into view, began to move forward.

"Sit down!" It was the other man. Borg stopped in his tracks.

"Turn him loose," Braden said quietly. "If the ape wants to try for seconds, I—"

"Never mind." The speaker held up a hand, looked at Borg. The heavy-set man sat down. The man who had spoken sat with feet crossed, a tall drink in his hand. He was a deeply tanned man, clad in sports shirt and tailored flannels, brown and white shoes. Sparse gray hair was carefully brushed over a tanned scalp, and he appeared to be about sixty.

"Grace saw the car lights, Mr. Braden. She didn't believe it could be you."

"What did you think?" Braden asked.

"I thought it could be." The man smiled, indicating the cluster of deck chairs. "Sit down. I know you've already met Mr. Borg and Mrs. Perin. The young lady goes by the improbable name of Gretchen Koori."

Braden nodded to long, bare legs—the rest of the figure was too deep in the shadowy canvas chair to see clearly. As he sat down, he noted Grace Perin had taken a chair near the older man and was sitting nervously on its edge.

"Drink, Braden? Our man makes excellent juleps."

"I'll drink some whiskey and water."

"Good." The man turned toward the door. "Wesley!"

A moment later Wesley Pierce came into the patio. His eyes slid over Braden, came to rest on the gray-haired man.

"Yes, sir?"

"Whiskey and water for Mr. Braden, Wesley. And make another round for the rest of us, please."

"Yes, sir."

As Pierce hurried off, the man turned to Braden. "I'm Clarence Samson."

Braden grinned crookedly. "Who else?"

Expensive dentures were revealed by a bare smile that didn't extend to muddy brown eyes. "All right, Mr. Braden. What is it you want?"

"Didn't you lose something, Samson?" Braden asked.

The dark eyes hooded, and the mouth became a scar. Samson leaned forward in his chair. "Yes, I lost something. Why?"

Braden settled back in his chair and smiled at the group. "I got it."

No one spoke for a long moment, then Grace Perin asked tensely: "Carol?"

"Carol, too." Braden looked up and saw Pierce approaching with the drinks. No one spoke until the houseman left.

"I told you, Clarence." It was the girl. She stood up and faced the older man. "I told you not to use a square broad, you stupid bastard!"

Braden had a chance to see her, now. He didn't believe it. What mixture of East and West could have produced Gretchen Koori? Dutch and Javanese? The Dutch made her big, certainly. Five-nine, at least, with silver-white hair falling to nearly mahogany shoulders—shoulders burnt black by the sun. She was dressed in the briefest of bikinis, the bandeau resting on impossible breasts. The exposed and swelling upper halves were startlingly white in comparison with the rest of her. She noticed Braden's stare, and slightly slanted green eyes flashed to him.

"I sell it, Braden, and you haven't got that much money."

Braden laughed aloud and looked at Samson. "You're quite a guy, Samson. A tired old dope fiend, a muscle-bound slob, and a whore. Your mob, man?"

A silence lay over the dimly lit patio. Finally Samson

spoke in a low voice. "You may be a dead man, Braden."

"Then what? What about your investment?"

"I told you! You should've—" Gretchen began.

"Shut up!" Samson hissed. "Shut up, you big slut, and sit down!" The girl blinked and sat down. Samson turned to Braden. "What do you want?"

"The film."

"How about my stuff?"

"I'll decide about that when I get the film. I might turn it over to the narco cops. I don't like dope."

Grace Perin broke in. "I told you. He's crazy."

"Keep quiet, Grace," Samson said coldly. "There's a lot of money involved, Braden, and you might get some of—"

Braden interrupted him. "I know how much junk you've got. It'll go roughly to eight times its basic price. That comes to nearly a quarter million, and I don't want any part of it."

"A hustler like you doesn't want money?" Samson asked, almost smiling.

"People have a feeling about dope, Samson. Even hustlers like me. So let's talk about the film. I got all the heroin and you're in no position to bargain."

"Where is it?" Samson asked.

Braden smiled, and noticed Gretchen Koori staring at him with murder in her eyes. Samson, hunching his shoulders, asked curiously:

"What makes you think I won't have you killed and to hell with the stuff, Braden?"

"Because you're not that big. You couldn't chance taking the loss. I'll bet it took every nickel you could scrape together to get into this deal, and you're an amateur in this large an operation." He looked around. "Sure. You're in a nice joint. A showplace. You have some good clothes, can speak English, are polite to the servants and can play lord of the manor. You know what? What you are is a nasty little smut peddler. Your front is too thin, you make me want to vomit, and do I get that film or not?"

"Just a minute—" Samson began, face livid.

"You asked me." Braden moved forward on his chair. "Now you'll listen to me."

"You can't talk—" Samson began again.

"Listen to him, Clarence," Gretchen said coldly.

Braden continued, "You've got no syndicate protection. Ordinarily, I'd worry about that, but not with you. I called around about you this evening. I talked to people who know if one little old lady spits on the sidewalk. These people never heard of you ever doing anything but making and selling dirty pictures for twisted old men." He mashed out his cigarette and waited for comment. There was none, and he went on.

"I think you stumbled into this, Samson. Carol Ashe and her background may have given you the idea. Or maybe Grace figured it out. You probably have enough connections to arrange for a buy in Mexico. It comes across uncut, straight to you. No syndicate to pay off, very little chance of getting tied into the buy—and an almost absolutely safe method of bringing it across. From you to the dealer, and you're home free." He took a drink; they were all listening, Samson with white lips.

"You worked it out like an amateur, Samson. First, you used Carol Ashe. Mistake number one. Gretchen is right. You shouldn't have used a square girl. She was hooked, but you still couldn't tell her anything about your plan. You had to let her ride on top of that heroin without her knowing it was there." He shook his head. "You ever figure what would have happened if she'd piled up on the road? With highway patrolmen investigating the accident? No . . . I guess not. The guy that pulled in front of the Mercedes at the border was a good idea. It drew the inspectors away from the girls. But the tail car showed me you had no syndicate connections. They would have had *two* cars following the Mercedes in case of a foul-up. They wouldn't have lost the girl. Not for any reason."

"The men in that car are still around, Braden," Samson said nastily. "They'd like to see you."

Braden ignored the older man's remark. "And who in

hell ever heard of bringing narcotics across in a white sports car?"

Borg and the two women were staring at Samson.

"They don't look as though they like it very much, boss man," Braden continued. "Don't feel bad. Maybe your biggest mistake was getting involved with them. Not even a cheap dirt dealer will fool with a dope addict. And then—"

Grace Perin stood up and left the patio without a backward glance.

"—And then there's Dutch." Braden looked at the squat man. "Big people don't have to use apes, Samson. This clown couldn't walk down the street with a Salvation Army lassie without being picked up by the law."

The big man stared at Braden with pig eyes, silently.

"Gretchen, I like." Braden smiled at the big girl and received a flat look in return. "I suppose she bought into the deal." He let his eyes run over her body. "She wouldn't have much trouble making the money. She's the only high card you're holding." He stopped talking, paid attention to his drink.

Samson's face was a mask of rigid anger. "All right, Braden. You've made your speech. I underestimated you. But I've made a few inquiries myself, and have found out a couple of things. I found out that you won't call the law. Ever. And that you won't interfere with another person's hustle. Right?"

"Okay, I won't blow a whistle. So?"

"So I want my stuff back. All of it. If you double-cross me you're finished. I may not be syndicate-connected, but I can buy your body and don't you forget it for a single minute." Samson indicated Borg with a nod of his head. "Dutch would enjoy taking care of you."

"I'll bet," Braden said expressionlessly.

"Then I guess we deal," Samson said.

"Do I get the film?"

"When I get the heroin."

Gretchen broke in again. "How do we know he won't swing with it?"

Samson didn't answer her.

"Well?" he asked.

"Okay," Braden said, "I'll trade with you."

"When can you bring it here?"

"Never. We make the exchange my way or no way."

Samson's eyes narrowed. "When?"

"I'll call you."

"How soon?" .

"Tomorrow, maybe. Or the day after." He stood and surveyed the three people. "I'll find my way out."

"Another drink?"

Braden shook his head. "I'm not that polite." He looked at Gretchen Koori, shook his head. "I don't believe it." Her glare had become speculative.

"Where are you staying?" Samson asked.

"Hollywood Roosevelt." Braden stared at the man. "Keep those creeps away from me. Tell 'em when this is over I'll be collecting—for that working over I got in the cemetery."

"Working over? I don't—"

"Never mind." Braden made his way to the front door, was ushered out by Wesley Pierce—who bowed politely, smiled nicely, and wished him good night.

CHAPTER **13**

THE sign said "L'Aiglon."

Braden turned into a long driveway and headed for the sprawling white stucco that lay a half-block deep in the large lot. He drove into a marked space provided by the management, left the car and approached the quiet building. Stark and ugly in bright daylight, Braden had seen it under operating conditions, covered by cosmetics of neon and night. It didn't look like a night club in the daytime.

He trotted up three wide steps, noting briefly that a song stylist entertained nightly. He paused by the darkened checkroom to glance in the full-length mirror. It was the day for the Sy Devore suit and bootmaker shoes so plain they had to be made from money.

The night before he'd checked into the Roosevelt for the second time. It had been after midnight when he'd gotten back from Palos Verdes. This morning he'd got up before noon, showered and shaved, and made a phone call. After the call he went through his luggage, then called valet service. He dressed carefully, ate breakfast in the hotel coffee shop, and shortly after noon, drove onto the Hollywood freeway. From the freeway he dropped into traffic-filled Ventura Boulevard, went through Studio City, Sherman Oaks, then began looking for the sign.

Now he looked at himself. The reflection satisfied him, and he moved into the club proper. Down two carpeted steps to the main room. He threaded his way through bare tables and empty chairs until he reached the tiny dance floor. He skirted it and went behind the orchestra dais, pushed aside heavy drapes and entered a hallway. The first door on his right was slightly ajar. He knocked.

"Come in!"

Braden entered and looked around expectantly.

"Over here, Stan."

Al Simon stood by an aquarium, gently tapping flakes of food into the water. He was gazing intently at the tiny, colorless fish gathered beneath the spreading food.

"My dealer stuck me for these," he explained, looking over his shoulder. "They cost a bundle, but they're rare. When they grow up they turn cannibalistic." He placed the food box at the side of the tank, then turned to face his visitor. He put out his hand. "How are you, Stan? Your call this morning surprised the hell out of me. What gives?"

The men shook hands.

"You can do something for me, Al."

"Sure. Come over and sit down." Simon led the way across the spacious office, showed Braden a chair, then went behind his desk and sat down. He was a big man, blond and vital. As he seated himself, his eyes came into startling view. They were flat blue and almost without expression in the reflected light of the canted Venetian blinds —a feature disconcerting to professional gamblers from coast to coast. He leaned forward and took rapid inventory of Braden's appearance.

"You look like you're out of the hole," he said.

"Clear out," Braden replied.

"Good. I heard you'd joined a carnival. Also heard you came up with a piece of the dough you owed."

Braden nodded. "I paid off five grand. The rest will be taken care of in a couple of days."

"Fine!" The blond man leaned back. "What you want from me?"

"First, I need a loan. Ten thousand."

"When do I get the money back?"

"In six months." Braden leaned forward. "I'm getting fifteen grand from another party, but I should have twenty-five to get started right."

"Okay. I'll let you have the ten. Now, what else?"

"I need a spot," Braden said.

The big man pursed his lips. "For lay-off action?"

"No. I'll book the stuff myself for a while. At least, until I get enough money to move farther back. What I need now is a place to go. It needs to be fixed good, and it needs to be away from this area. I can't stand any more courtroom scenes."

"You're handing me a big order." The club owner opened a box and removed a cigar. He pushed the box toward Braden, who declined. Simon prepared the cigar and lit it, then studied the man opposite him. "It won't be so easy to—"

"All right," Braden said, reaching for a cigarette. "It's a big order, but I need it. If you can't, you can't, and you can forget about the—" He started to rise.

"Sit down, sit down." Simon waved the cigar, frowning. "God-damn, you're touchy. I'll get you a spot. A good one." He leaned forward and smiled. "You've sent a buck or two in my direction."

"You don't owe me," Braden said irritably.

"Then we'll call it a favor," Simon said. He rubbed his chin thoughtfully. "I'll have to make some calls and maybe see a couple of people. Then you'll have to see 'em. When can you be ready?"

"In a few days." Braden rose. "Suppose I call you Saturday sometime?"

"After six." Simon stood and reached his hand across the desk. "Glad to see you back in business, Stan. Why didn't you come to me before?"

"Could you have loaned me ten thousand dollars when I was twelve thousand dollars in the hole?"

"Oh. Yeah." Simon came from behind the desk and began to walk Braden to the front of the club. "Well, anyway, I'm still glad you're back and hope you make another bundle." They reached the front of the building and stood outside the entryway for a moment.

"You like the action, don't you, Stan?" the owner asked.

"I like money."

"Same thing. Everything first-cabin and when you want it." Simon shook his head.

"Don't knock it," Braden said. "I remember you rigging games with both hands."

"Yeah, I did." Simon puffed contentedly on the cigar. "Now I sort of like the saloon business. And being a post office for you people. No hassle and no crazy losers to worry about. What I got is mine and no strings attached to any of it."

"Al the barkeep, huh?" Braden smiled at the man. "Okay. It's your red wagon. Me, I know where I'm going. All you got to do is put me on the road and point me." He walked down the steps. "See you, Al."

He drove back to Hollywood and parked in the hotel parking lot. In the lobby he started for the elevators, then changed his mind. He walked into the hotel bar.

An hour later he sat hunched over a drink, thinking of money. Twenty-five grand. No more scratching for peanuts in a cheap tent show. With the money from Ashe and Simon, he had it. Identity. Stan Braden, the book. Status. The man who could walk in and never ask the price. The boy with the juice. The guy who could keep the payola fixed, the law happy. With a retinue of sharp young men and a couple of lovely ladies to . . . He looked at his empty glass irritably, tapped the bar. Four highballs since he'd come back from Simon's. Five, if you counted the one just ordered.

He picked up the drink, then turned halfway on his stool and surveyed the room. The Cinegrill. What was the saying around Hollywood? Something about if you meet in the Cinegrill, you . . .

"Hello, bastard." The words were whispered in his ears. From behind. He could smell musky perfume, feel hair tickle his neck. He took a deep drink and turned around.

Gretchen Koori. She was leaning back now, one elbow on the bar, one hip on the stool. A position that made her figure more impossible than ever. She wore a white coat. Plain, and held together in front, it covered everything but tanned legs. Her silver hair blended into the flared collar. A score of male patrons arrested their drinking arms and looked at her. Green eyes looked brazenly into Braden's, and small white teeth glistened between carmined lips.

"You buying, Braden?" She asked it in a normal tone.

"A drink?"

"This is a bar, isn't it?" Incredibly long nails rested for a moment on his sleeve. "Please, tiger."

Braden motioned to the bartender. She ordered a double Scotch on the cubes. When it arrived, she drank it. Then she pushed the empty glass toward the man in the white jacket, tapped on it with a cerise nail. The second drink she picked up and held.

"Thanks."

"Sure." Braden drank more of his highball, then leaned closer to the girl. "What you doin' here, doll? Meeting a customer?"

"No," she said calmly, smiling at him. "I came to see you."

"The ape know you're out?"

"I buy people like Dutch. Besides, he belongs to Samson."

"Okay." He shifted position. "You've seen me."

"I want to talk." The nails showed on the sleeve again. "Business."

Braden drained the glass and stood up. He felt the five

tall ones slightly but didn't weave. "What kind of business have you and I got?"

She slid from the bar stool and took his arm. The coat did nothing to disguise the pressure of a munificent breast. Braden dug a bill from his pocket, glanced at it and tossed it on the bar. When he turned to face her, her eyes were almost even with his.

"I asked you a question," he said.

"Do I have to answer it here?"

"Where else?"

"How about your room?" She tugged on his arm, and they moved toward the lobby. He stopped her near the elevators.

"Samson know you're here?"

She laughed.

"No, huh?" He moved forward. "Okay, c'mon up."

CHAPTER **14**

INSIDE his room the girl flopped in an armchair as he walked to the window and pulled aside the curtains, disclosing busy Hollywood Boulevard below. He went to the telephone and called room service, ordered a fifth of Scotch and setups. She watched him move around the room, finally crooked a finger when he finished with the phone.

"Come here."

He walked around her chair and leaned over the back. She raised her arms and placed a hand on either side of his face, drawing him down.

It was a long kiss, and expert. Whatever could be done, she did. She finally let him go, pushed him away.

"A sample. Now sit on the bed. I want to talk."

He did as she asked, folded his arms and waited.

"Were you serious about only wanting the film?" she asked. She leaned forward and did things to the front of the coat.

"That's right."

Her beautiful mouth twisted. "They tell me you were big, Braden. A lay-off bookie. What happened? Your head get soft when they broke you?"

Braden didn't move, said quietly, "I don't like dope."

"You're sitting on nearly a quarter million bucks' worth of narcotics and you're sniveling about morals. You haven't any other ideas?" She pulled a package of cigarettes from her coat pocket, extracted one and put it in her mouth. She let it hang insolently until he flicked his lighter and held the flame under it. "Or maybe you're afraid Carol's old man will get a load of that film before it hits the stag circle. You should see it, Braden. What Samson couldn't think of, I did. We got the camera in real—"

Braden slapped her with the hand holding the lighter. The force of the blow almost knocked her from the chair. Silver hair swirled about her face amid sparks from the crushed cigarette. She straightened slowly, hands clutching the arms of the chair, then pushed her hair back from about her face. Ashes smudged her chin. She smiled and ran the tip of her tongue over her smeared lips.

"That's my boy," she said softly. "For a minute I—"

"How much film has he got?" Braden asked her.

"Four cans," she answered sullenly.

"Negatives?"

"One set of negatives and one set of prints. That's all he'll have until he gets some more money. But I didn't come here to talk about—"

She was interrupted by a knock on the door. Braden answered it and let the bellman enter with the liquor. As soon as he and the girl were alone again, he made them drinks. He handed her one.

"Tell me what you have to say," he said.

"All right, here it is." Gretchen Koori looked at him over her glass and watched him drink deeply. "Samson's been making flesh pictures for years. He's gotten to know a few people. So he finally meets a guy who can set up a buy in Mexico." She shrugged. "The Ashe kid was wandering around at the right time. Either Perin or Samson thought up the idea of sending her to Mexico to pick it up. I don't know which. Anyway, he's going to peddle the stuff to a couple of big dealers here, take his cut, and back off." She crossed her long legs and looked at him.

"So? I told you all that at Palos Verdes." He finished his drink, felt the Scotch flood through his body. "How come you're up here playing footsie with me?" He left the bed and made another highball. As he stood, watching the girl, he felt the first signs of real drunkenness wash over him. "How much was your share going to be?"

"Half. Samson and Perin had half the cash, and I came up with the rest."

"How come they let you in?"

"They had to." She got up from the chair and walked to the window. She talked with her back to him. "I know everything there is to know about both of them. What they're in, I'm in. Now they're not in. You are. You need a map, Braden?"

"Tell me."

She pulled the curtains over the blinds, putting the room in semidarkness, then said evenly, "Let's take it all. Sell it."

Braden stared at the girl's back. "You're sweet. What happens to Carol? Does she go on the dirty-picture circuit?"

She whirled around, lips curling. "Who are you to worry about giving a break, carny? Do you protect the suckers? You'd take the last quarter from a sharecropper across that roll-down counter of yours."

"I have." He belted another inch of highball. "You've been asking around, huh?"

"I've been asking."

"Their money I took. I didn't mess with their lives." The words came thickly.

"Crap!" She walked over and stood in front of him, feet apart, hands in the pockets of the coat. "Carol's on dope, Braden. How much chance do you think she has of staying clean? You know the odds. Listen! You want back on top, don't you? I know where that heroin can be dropped for at least half of its value. That's over a hundred grand." Her eyes narrowed. "I want that kind of money."

He sat on the edge of the bed and leaned back on his elbows, glass in hand. "You're crazy. Samson isn't much, but he'd have me killed. Quick."

"No!" She sat down beside him. "Not if you're not around. He probably could have it done here. Dutch, maybe. But he doesn't have the money or the connections to have it done by remote control." She unloosened his tie, unbuttoned his shirt collar. "He's an old man. All you wind up with is a suitcase full of money."

He sat up, moving away from the questing fingers. He took another drink. A hundred grand. The sound of the figures tasted good. He looked at the girl and grabbed a handful of silver hair. He twisted her down until she had to look up at him.

"And what's your cut?" He held her that way until he saw white teeth show in the tanned face. She didn't answer until he let her go. Then she sat up and shook out her hair.

"Half. Right down the center. And I go with you to peddle it."

Braden sat up straight, shook his head from side to side. "I got to think. I told you I don't like dope."

"What's to think?" Gretchen Koori stood up, faced him. "You don't have to like it. Just sell it." She smiled. "Half, Braden."

"That's all?"

"And me," she amended. She walked to the window, pulled the cord to open the Venetian blinds behind the curtains. Sunlight filtered through the brocade drapes, dappled the room with light and shadow. She unbuttoned the coat and tossed it on the chair.

Braden blinked.

She wasn't quite naked. The white coat had covered the same bikini he'd seen the night before. In the light-streaked room it could barely be discerned. She moved in front of him and laughed softly.

"I come with the deal." She looked down at her body, then squared her shoulders until the upper half of the bikini was stretched taut. He stood and went to the bureau, poured himself another drink.

"What do I do with you?" He was weaving now.

"That's easy." She walked toward him as though she were on a runway. "I'll be yours, Braden. Until you get tired. Then give me my cut and I'll get out of your way." She stopped, almost touching him.

He stared at the woman, then pulled her close and savagely kissed her. She took one of his hands, led it to the knot between her shoulders. He untied it. Still pressed tight against him, she guided his other hand to a swelling hip.

"Untie that one, too," she said into his mouth. He did.

When she stepped back, two pieces of cloth fell to the floor.

"Well, come on . . . tiger!" she said.

Churning liquor fumes woke him. He was facing the open window and saw it was dark outside. He turned over slowly and snapped on the bed lamp, then glanced at his watch. 9:30 P.M. He swung his legs over the side of the bed, put his head in his hands and tried to remember when Gretchen had left. He couldn't.

In the bathroom he stared at his reflection in the medicine-cabinet mirror, scowled at it, then stepped into the stall shower. Under the needlelike spray he thought it over.

It hadn't worked out. Maybe she ruined it, or maybe it was the combination of too much liquor, cloying perfume and heavy flesh. He could remember she had been an animal. A voluptuous, frustrated animal. Then she'd left him alone.

Why in hell should she leave? He dried off, walked into the bedroom and sat on the edge of the bed. No one as money-hungry as Gretchen Koori would have left before it was settled one way or another. He frowned, scratched his shoulder.

A fine deal, Braden. Fifty grand and a woman. All you have to do is put your life on the line, toss Carol Ashe to the wolves, and flood Los Angeles with heroin. And what about the girl from Atwater? What would she think of . . . He shook his head and began to dress.

He reached for a suit, choosing the one he'd left at Jean Webster's. As he started to tear off the cleaner's bag, he stopped suddenly. The pink ticket, with Jean's name and address on it, was gone.

Braden grabbed the phone and dialed the Citrus number. He heard it ring twice, then heard the receiver lifted and waited for one of the girls to speak. All he could hear was breathing, then a click as the connection was broken. He slammed down the phone and finished dressing rapidly.

He rushed downstairs, almost ran to his car. Then cursed audibly all the way down Sunset to Vermont, holding the Ford to a reasonable speed. He didn't dare take a chance of being stopped. A look at his watch showed him it was not quite ten. The Koori woman already had two hours to do whatever she was going to do. It seemed forever before he reached Atwater.

He left the car a full block from the house, then kept to the shadows as he made his way on foot. Only one light was visible when he arrived at the house. It could barely be seen through the closed blinds of Jean Webster's room. He moved toward the rear of the house.

As he passed the lighted room, he thought he heard a strangled cry. He hurried to the back door. It wasn't locked.

He entered the house quietly and moved through the kitchen. Sounds of television were coming from the front room, the volume normal. He crossed the dark dining room and noted the picture tube was on. A late passer-by would note nothing unusual. The bedroom door was slightly ajar, light showing at the narrow opening. He moved quickly and peered in.

Jean Webster sat in an armchair, partially facing the door. Her wrists were taped to the arms of the chair, ankles to the legs. She was gagged, a small trickle of blood coming from the corner of the gag. Fully clothed in skirt and sweater, she was staring in disbelief at the bed. Braden shifted his position to see better.

They had Carol Ashe spread-eagled on the bed, wrists and ankles tied to the posts with stockings. She too, was gagged, completely dressed except for shoes and stockings.

Face covered with perspiration, eyes rolling wildly, her head was moving doggedly from side to side. The little man stood at the head of the bed.

"Tell it, girl." He grabbed her hair and forced her to look at him. "If you want to tell me where it is, nod your head. You don't, he lights the lighter."

The larger man was bending over her bare feet. From Braden's position he could see only the tops of her toes. On her right foot, near the little toe, he could see soot marks. He braced himself, placed his hands on the edge of the door and the door frame.

"All right. One more time." The little man nodded to the man at the foot of the bed. The lighter was flicked, and Carol's head began to move faster. A muffled moan came through the gag.

Braden burst through the door. The big man's head jerked in startled movement as Braden's first stride carried him halfway to the foot of the bed. The second step saw his right foot arch forward. All of his weight drove in a straight line, shoulder to toe, catching the man half-turned to face him. The hand, lighter and shoe mashed into the broad face together, and the man flew backward to crash into the wall.

Braden didn't stop moving, allowed himself to fall sideways on the edge of the bed. He bounced up in time to grasp the little man's wrist as it came from a coat pocket. The forty-five was held in the hand that followed. Braden stabbed spread fingers deep in the man's eyes and bore down on the thin wrist. The little man mewed in agony, clutched at his eyes with his free hand. A split second later his wrist snapped, jerking a scream from deep within him. Before it could reach his lips, the edge of a hard hand struck his throat, silenced him, and the barrel of the automatic pounded against his head as he dropped to the floor.

By this time, the big man was attempting to rise from the floor. Blood poured from his nose and mouth and covered his ruined face. His chin was laid open to the bone, and he was climbing to his feet on instinct alone. Braden stepped quickly to his side, used the automatic again. The man slumped to the carpet with a tired sigh.

Braden cut Carol Ashe loose first, then Jean. The girl in the chair looked up at him with naked wildness in her eyes as he loosed the gag. She could only whisper his name as the bonds were being cut loose. She started to say something, looked instead at Carol. The Ashe girl was holding her foot with both hands, sobbing hysterically. Jean stumbled to the bed and held the auburn-haired girl tightly.

Braden bound the men with the stockings that had been used on Carol. He used their own handkerchiefs for gags. Both were breathing noisily, still unconscious. He leaned over Carol's foot, pulled aside her hands and examined the burns. He cursed monotonously until Jean interrupted him.

"Call the police!" She still held the tortured girl tightly in her arms.

He shook his head. "Can't." He nodded at Carol. "Keep her as quiet as you can. We can't afford to have the law in here. Fix her foot and give her a big drink. You'd better have one yourself." He looked toward the bound men. They'd begun to stir. "I'm taking this garbage out of here. I'll be back as soon as I dump it."

Jean's eyes were filled with shock and anger. Braden stepped to the side of the bed and grasped her shoulder. She looked up at him.

"Come out of it," he said harshly. "It's all over and this girl needs attention. I'll be back before you know it." He looked at her closely. "Did either of these men do anything to you or Carol?"

Awareness came into the shocked eyes. "No," she said, then looked back at Carol. "I'll take care of her."

Braden jerked the groggy men to their feet, herded them to the back door and out onto the rear lawn. In the comparative darkness there, he placed the forty-five against the small man's neck.

"All right, little man, where is she?" He jammed the automatic into flesh. "Remember what you told me? One sound, friend. One sound, and I beat your head off with this iron." He pulled the gag loose with his free hand.

"She's in the car," the man chattered hoarsely. "Around the corner and up a block. Look, Braden, if you'll—"

Braden shoved the gag back in the man's mouth. "I'll follow you. Both of you. Keep to the shadows and you'd damned well better walk soft!"

He followed the men closely, finally saw the dark sedan parked between two street lights. He halted the men, peered through the darkness at the car. Silver hair was visible through the rear window.

"Walk to the car real slow," he ordered, nudged the men forward with the gun. They were almost to the open window before she saw them. Her lips parted, eyes widened in surprised fear.

"Don't say it," Braden warned. "One word, you lousy bitch, and I'll change your face." He let her look into the muzzle of the automatic. "I should anyway."

She looked at the bloody faces of the two bound men, turned back to Braden. He shoved the men closer to the car window.

"What are their names?" he asked.

Gretchen Koori licked her lips, her eyes beginning to narrow. Braden reached in the car, put the gun close to her face.

"I asked you a question."

"You can't shoot anyone out here, Braden. If you—" The words ended in a choked cry as the barrel of the forty-five was flicked lightly against her lips and teeth. The weight of the big automatic did damage. Pain flooded the green eyes, and she put both hands to her mouth. The bound men watched her impassively.

"Their names." Braden watched red seep between her fingers.

"Benjy Reed and Art Fowler," she said brokenly. She lowered her hands, tried to see herself in the rearview mirror.

"Benjy the little one?"

She nodded, fear still apparent in the green eyes.

"Okay. Let 'em in the car."

She opened the door and let the men squeeze in behind her. They flopped clumsily in the back seat, then sat quietly.

"You'll have a dental bill," Braden said to Gretchen. He leaned on the window sill. "Now, listen. I know all your names and I'll lay odds that you all have records. I'm giving your names to the girl that lives back there. She'll call the police if I let her, and being a square girl with a clean background, she could settle you all. For a long time. Aggravated assault with great bodily harm can put you all in prison." He paused, spoke slowly. "If any one of you gets near me again, ever, the blond girl calls the law." He looked at the woman's face, then at the two men in the back seat. "You'd better drive somewhere and put a foot through the windshield. Then go to a hospital and tell 'em you were in a wreck. You can all use some stitches."

As he stepped back, Gretchen Koori started the engine.

"Oh, yeah." Braden leaned forward again. "You'd better leave this part of the country, doll."

Her head turned in his direction.

"Yeah," he continued. "I'm telling Samson about you. I guess he'll be interested."

He stepped back quickly, barely avoided the car as it roared away from the curb. He watched it until it turned toward Glendale Boulevard. He didn't anticipate further trouble from Gretchen Koori and her helpers.

He turned and retraced his steps to the house.

CHAPTER **15**

"Hi, Stan. Did you clobber 'em?"

Carol Ashe lay on the bed, eyes open and pain-clouded. She managed a wan smile.

He nodded briefly. "They won't be back." He walked to the bed and looked down at her. "You hurting?"

"Some." She grimaced, turned her head on the crumpled pillow so she could look directly at him. "You'd better find

Jean. She was shaking terribly when she put the salve on
my foot. I can't tell whether she's just plain mad or terrified."

Braden looked about the room. Torn adhesive tape lit-
tered the floor, spots of blood showing on the bleached,
white rug. He bent over, scooped the girl up in his arms
and carried her to the other bedroom. After placing her on
the bed, he let one hand rest on the side of her face.

"I'm sorry they hurt you," he said quietly.

Carol put a hand over his and smiled. "I'm not. Really.
Right now I should be tearing myself apart for some help."
She looked up at him. "You know the kind of help I mean.
But I'm not, and that's good. Anyway, it wasn't your fault,
Stan."

"Wasn't it?" he said bitterly, thinking of the hotel room
and Gretchen Koori.

"You'd better go to Jean. I'll be all right."

Braden pulled his hand away slowly. "You're a good girl,
Carol. Herndon's lucky."

Jean Webster was sitting on the divan, hands clasped
whitely in her lap. She hardly noticed Braden when he
entered. He sat next to her and reached for her hands; they
were ice cold. She was dressed in the white pajamas and the
blue robe.

"He tore my skirt and sweater," she explained through
pale lips.

"Who?" Braden asked.

"The big man." She looked straight ahead as she talked.
"We had been to a movie up in Glendale, and when we
got home they were waiting in the house for us. I don't
know how they got in. The little man stuck a gun in Carol's
stomach, and when I started to scream, the big man hit
me." The girl pulled one hand loose and touched the corner
of her mouth with a finger. "He put me in the chair," she
said, words rushing out, "and tied me to it. Covered my
mouth with adhesive tape. Then he put his hands all over
me, Mr. Braden, and talked about my body." The girl began
to shake but said angrily, "The little man had to make
him stop."

Braden slid one arm behind her knees, the other around her shoulders. He picked her up, walked to the leather chair and sat down with her in his arms. He started talking.

"All right, kid. All right. They're gone and they won't come back. You've had something happen to you that you don't want to believe." He looked down at her. "Try not to think about it."

He kept on talking, softly and soothingly. About anything and everything. He told her she wasn't really hurt and that nothing had been done that couldn't be undone. He talked about Pete Herndon and Carol Ashe; about Mario; finally about himself. He talked for nearly an hour.

He told her about the early years in the carnival and Step Halvorsen. How he'd learned all the gimmicks and how he'd used them. And why. About the studies and the reading, the reasons they were necessary. Then he talked about the prison and Clayton Ashe. Then about how he wanted to write, but didn't figure he had the time—or the talent.

Slowly, the rigid body relaxed. In one movement, she clutched at his jacket, buried her face hard into his shirt.

He explained about the first small bookie action, the bigger lay-off operation. The trips to Europe, the cars, the expensive hotels. He painted the big life and told her he'd be able to buy it again. He didn't say how.

The girl finally pushed herself away from him. "Please let me up."

"You okay?"

"Let me up, please. I want to blow my nose." She slid from his lap and walked unsteadily to the dining room. She found a handkerchief in the pocket of the robe and used it. A moment later she came back to stand in front of him.

"I'm all right now." She pushed the ottoman in front of the chair with a bare foot and sat down. She faced him, elbows on her knees. "How is Carol?" she asked.

"Resting. I put her in your father's room."

She nodded, then put a hand on his knee and looked up

at him. The top button of the pajama coat had become un-
fastened while he'd been holding her, disclosing a soft throat
and part of a white shoulder. She smiled a little.

"Haven't you anything to say to me, Mr. Braden?"

All he did was pull her to him and hold her close. He
put his face against a bare, clean shoulder and forgot about
policemen, Palos Verdes, narcotics and greedy, silver-haired
women.

After a while she slid her arms around his neck and began
kissing him. Her lips were warm and frank under his. She
leaned back.

"You knew I loved you?"

He nodded.

"I knew you loved me, too." She kissed him again, let
her upper body rest closely against his. "With me it started
the morning you cured my hang-over. How about you?"

He shook his head helplessly and didn't answer. Just
held her. She finally stirred in his arms, looked up and
smiled shyly.

"You look terrible, Stan. I'll make us some coffee. Probably Carol will want some, too."

"Okay, kid." He pushed her to her feet, followed her into
the kitchen, then stood watching as she filled the percolator
and plugged it in. When she'd finished, she turned to face
him, brown eyes softly warm.

"Do you like this house, Stan?"

"Why, sure," he said. "I don't know much about houses,
but—"

"It's comfortable and all the furniture is mine," she broke
in happily. "We could fix up my father's room as a study
for you to do your writing and, what with my job, it wouldn't
be too hard for us to—"

"Now, see here," he interrupted quickly. "You know how
I feel about that writing business. I'm not sure that I can
cut it. Besides, I can't be tied down to one place in my
kind of operation. You know that."

She looked puzzled, the happy smile beginning to fade.
"Your type of operation? Surely you're not planning to go

on with bookmaking, are you?" Her voice rose slightly. "Do you think it's a very respectable kind of work? After what it's gotten you into?"

"Just a minute!" Braden said. "You can't—"

"Well, do you?" she asked angrily, her eyes glinting dangerously. "Look what happened here tonight. Is that part of—" She stopped suddenly, face flushed. "Just what *were* those men after?"

Braden stared at her a moment. "I can't tell you," he said simply. "Forget it."

"Forget it?" Jean Webster stepped back and looked at him in amazement. "What's the matter with you? Two men come into my house, torture that girl in there, manhandle me, and you say 'forget it'! I want to know what they wanted," she said angrily.

"It doesn't make any difference to you. As soon—"

"It does!" She pulled the robe tighter about her, then looked at him with blazing eyes. "I know you must have a reason for not calling the police. I've gone along with that because I've trusted you. But I'm not going one step further unless you tell me what's going on. I may be naïve, but I'm not stupid, Stan. I won't stumble around in this any longer. Either you tell me, or I'm going to call the police."

"You'd better tell her, Stan." It was Carol Ashe.

They both looked toward the door separating the kitchen from the dining room and saw the auburn-haired girl standing there. She limped toward them, glanced at the coffeepot, and sat on the kitchen stool, putting her sore foot up on a near-by chair.

Braden looked from one girl to the other, shrugged his shoulders. He sat down in one of the kitchen chairs, flung an arm over the back. "All right," he said, looking at Jean. "How much has Carol told you?"

"Not much," Jean replied. "Just that you got her away from some people who had made her ill."

"Tell her," Braden ordered the Ashe girl.

"It was narcotics, Jean," Carol Ashe said evenly. "Dope. Heroin, to be exact. I'm an addict." She hesitated. "Or was."

"Oh!" Jean gave Braden a look of dismay, then turned and got cups and saucers from a cabinet and placed them on the table. She went over to the coffeepot, brought it to the table and poured the steaming brew. Then she took a place at the chrome-stripped table.

In a low voice Carol told Jean the story. She omitted only the part about the film. When she finished, Jean turned to Braden.

"But why didn't you tell me, Stan? If I'd known that—"

Braden shook his head. "It wasn't my story to tell."

"I'm glad you got her away and helped her so much in that cabin," Jean said, "but I still want to know why those men kept asking her, 'where is it?' "

"I don't know, either," Carol said, looking at Braden. "I tried to tell him every time he took the gag away, but he wouldn't believe me."

"All right. I'll tell you." Braden drank some of his coffee. "How much money did you turn over to the guy in Ensenada?" he asked Carol.

"Almost twenty thousand dollars. At least, that's what I was told. I never opened the package."

"Do you know what the money was for?" he asked.

"No. Samson said it was business."

"I'll bet he did." Braden grunted. "You brought two kilos of pure heroin over in that white car of yours. It was taped under the running gear. They probably put it there while the car was in that garage in Ensenada." He looked at Carol. "Two kilos. That's over four pounds."

"Oh, God!" Carol Ashe had turned white during his last speech. "What if they'd stopped me at the border? And Peggy . . ." She stopped, and stared with dawning realization at Braden. "No wonder you wanted to get her out of that restaurant."

"What does it mean?" Jean asked.

Braden turned to her. "It means a quarter of a million dollars at retail prices. It means people are waiting to pay Samson for delivery. And if I don't deliver it all to him, it means he'll be after me."

"That means he'll try and have you killed, doesn't it?" Jean Webster said, quietly.

"Probably," he said.

"Have you got it, Stan?" Carol asked.

"I have it." He drank from the coffee cup, stared unseeingly across the edge of it. All were silent for a moment, then Jean broke in.

"But, Stan, you *can't* give it back!"

"What can I do?" Braden said.

"You can destroy it. Turn it over to the police."

"He can't, Jean." Carol placed her cup in the saucer and faced the blond girl. She told her about the motion-picture film.

"You see how it is?" Braden said, when Carol had finished. "Either I give it back or Carol is in trouble. Or I get myself killed." He leaned back in his chair. "Samson's not very big, but he can afford to have me wiped out. And he would, for over a hundred thousand dollars." He leaned forward, spread both hands on the table and looked at Jean. "I'm sorry you're involved."

Carol excused herself and limped out of the kitchen. Braden glanced at the kitchen clock and stood up.

"Late," he said. "I'd better get started for—"

"Please stay, Stan." Jean put a hand on his arm. "We'd feel a lot better if you were here in the house for the rest of the night."

He looked down at her. "Sure, kid. I'll go in and wash up. Then I can flop on—"

"I'll fix you a bed on the divan," she broke in, starting for the front room.

"Never mind the bed," he said. "Just bring me a blanket."

The girl turned. "It's no trouble—"

"Just a blanket." He headed for the bathroom.

Later, in the dark front room, he lay staring at the dim ceiling. He heard a door open and shut in the still house. A moment later, Jean Webster padded into the room and sat on the edge of the divan.

"I couldn't sleep," she said.

"You still mad?"

"No, I guess not."

"You need the rest," he said.

"Yes." She twisted around and lay down beside him. He covered both of them with the blanket. The girl's breath mingled with his, and she threw her arm across his chest. "I guess I'm yours now," she whispered.

He didn't answer.

"Before the night's over you can make sure I belong to—"

"Look, you just don't ask—"

"I do too!" she said fiercely. "I'm almost twenty-six years old and I haven't done a damned thing in my whole life." She tightened the arm across his chest, pressed close. "Please."

He lay there, felt the pounding of her heart.

"Stan?"

"Yeah?"

"I didn't mean to be so forward."

"You were. From you it doesn't sound right."

"I know." She pushed herself up until her face loomed over his. "I don't know very much," she said. She placed soft palms on each side of his face, let herself down to meet his mouth. Her hands slipped around to dig into his neck. She ran her fingers over his lips and eyes when the kiss was over, then kissed his neck, finally burying her face there.

"I didn't know it could be this way," she breathed, then kissed him again, her mouth half-parted. This time his hands spread across her back, pressing her to him. She pulled her mouth away, her brown eyes shining in the dark. "The day you put your hand on my bare back. Please show me—" She put her face against his neck again, whispered, "Be careful with me, Stan."

Braden sat up abruptly, almost knocking the girl to the floor. He pushed her aside, got up and turned on a lamp. She lay back on the divan and stared at him.

"Listen to this," he said harshly. He reached out and pulled her to a sitting position. He looked at the pajama coat. She had unbuttoned it in the darkness. "And button up that goddamned coat!"

Her fingers flew to the buttons, face fiery as she tried to fasten them.

"You feel it's all right if I take the heroin back?" He sat down in the big chair.

"Yes." Her voice trembled.

"Because it's the only way out?"

She nodded.

"You didn't seem very happy about my going back into business. Making book." He leaned back in the chair, grasped the arms.

"I'd prefer it if you'd try the writing. But I sup—"

"No." He shook his head stubbornly. "I might not make it and I might have to give up too much time for nothing. No one gives up anything for nothing," he said. "Me included."

"I was just about to," she said quietly.

"I'm going to get where I want to go," he said, ignoring what she'd said. He looked at her. "You can go with me if you want to. But no more lousy carnivals, no cheap clothes—" He looked around, blurted out, "—no cheap neighborhoods."

Jean Webster sat up straighter, eyes beginning to glint dangerously. "And where will the money come from?" she asked. "Won't getting started again take a considerable amount of money?"

"Plenty. But I'll have enough."

"From what Mr. Ashe pays you?"

"Not exactly," he said evasively. "I have another source, and I—"

"Another source!" she said in amazement. "How? You've told me you're still deeply in debt. Who would back you under those con—" She stopped suddenly, a hand flying to her mouth. "Samson! You're going to *sell* the heroin back to Samson!"

"Hold it!" he began. "I'm not—"

"How *could* you, Stan? You can't start a new life by

using money from that dirty stuff. Why, it would be like blood money."

"Now, wait a—"

"A man that would take that sort of money would do anything," she cut in wildly. "How could I marry a man who—"

"Who asked you?" he interrupted savagely. He watched the girl clutch her stomach as though she'd been hit, then went on: "What do you want from me? I haven't made any—" He stopped, looked at her. Tears had forced themselves over her eyelids and were coursing down her cheeks. Finally he spoke in a dead voice. "Just go to bed, kid, and leave me alone. I'll get Carol out of here tomorrow."

Jean got up and walked toward her bedroom without a backward glance. He heard the door close, then open again. She came to the dining-room door. She stood there and looked at him, tears running down her cheeks.

"In some ways you've been a good man, Mr. Braden," she said through quivering lips. "But you didn't have to hurt me, and I think you're a son-of-a-bitch!"

CHAPTER **16**

". . . AND these bums tell me they're going to void my contract, and I tell 'em to go ahead and void already, 'cause they'll have to pay through the nose. Plenty. So, they . . ."

Braden tried to shut out the whiny voice, heard another instead. Son-of-a-bitch, son-of-a-bitch, son-of . . . It drummed in his ears until it became a litany. He leaned over his beer and tried not to hear it.

He was in The Pig, and it suited him. He'd driven there directly from Jean Webster's, knowing the bar opened at six o'clock in the morning.

He contemplated his flattened beer and called for another. He pointed to the empty shot glass at the same time. The bartender served him, rang up the sale, then went back to the woman with the querulous voice. Braden tossed down the bar whiskey, washed it down with a drink of beer. He looked around, then looked at his watch. Six-thirty.

From time to time, an early morning worker would come through the front door, place a metal lunch box on the bar; a couple of quick belts and off to work. Braden turned on the stool and looked out at the almost deserted street. An occasional car or truck went by, the short rows of glasses on the back bar rattling at the passage. A fit place for him—without meaning and without pleasure.

". . . and who the hell can't get pregnant, I says to 'em. It's easy, I says, and all you got to do is wait and we'll shoot the exterior scenes around me until . . ." The whining lowered.

He finally ran out of places to look and had to face the bar mirror. Stan Braden. His hat was shoved back on his head, face harsh under the cheap fluorescent lights. He stared too long, then whirled on the stool and moved to the pinball machines. He started feeding coins to one of the brightly illuminated gimmicks and wished it would get late enough to call Samson and get the exchange started.

Who in hell did Jean Webster think she was? He pulled out the plunger, let it hit home. What right did she have, jumping to conclusions, figuring he was going to sell the dope back to Samson? As if he would peddle . . . He thought of the silver-haired girl in his hotel room. Maybe if he hadn't been so full of booze, she could have talked him into stealing the stuff. Maybe it had been in the back of his mind all the time. It was easy to think about going for the big money.

And why shouldn't he sell it back to Samson? The mindless escapists who bought it would find it somewhere. A protected girl from a small town couldn't be expected to know the world was mostly a bad place, that when you took a chance you were expected to collect for it. Anyway, it was probably a good thing she got mad. How could she fit into the life he had planned for himself? But what to do with the heroin? The little steel balls came bouncing down through the obstacles, missing the pay-off numbers. No bells rang.

After he'd found the girl at the Perin house he should have bulled his way in and gotten her. He might have been able to get the film from Samson some other way. Then there wouldn't have been any Mexico or hijacking of dope. No problems. He'd caused those by doing it the cute way.

He'd caused the girl to get her feet burned. He'd been the reason the big man put his hands on Jean Webster. He bit on the thought as it formed—smart Stan Braden. The words tasted bitter in his mouth.

He knew now he had never seriously thought about stealing the heroin or selling it back. Now he didn't even like the idea of giving it back. How in hell could he get that film without dealing with Samson? As he had told the girls, keeping it or throwing it away would bring an inevitable bullet. He roughly jacked another steel ball into the trough, pulled back on the plunger.

". . . and I tell 'em, you'll not pay off, hell. You don't come up with the full contract figure and I'll throw the Act of God clause on you. You shoulda seen 'em, Harry. The whole damned bunch of 'em backed off like . . ."

The plunger didn't spring forward. Braden held it for a moment, staring at the multicolored lights on the face of the ornate play device. He finally allowed it to come to rest softly, didn't jack the remaining balls into the playing slot. He walked back to the bar and picked up his beer, then made his way slowly to the rear of the line of stools. He looked at the owner of the whiny voice.

She was a faded woman—faded eyes and hair. She had coarse, brittle hair, the original color lost forever beneath much dye and many rinses, with dark roots and varicolored ends. A dumpy figure, sagging under a flowered dress of garden-party mode. She wore costume jewelry and a big hat. He recognized her for what she was. One of the brigade. Too far gone to bother Central Casting any longer. Veined hands and worn feet—nothing left but memories and thirst. She was nursing a beer, looked up at his approach.

"What you drinking, lady?"

"I usually drink bourbon," she said regally and with diction. She was old enough to remember when women bridled, tried it until she realized how ridiculous it was, then slumped again over her beer.

Braden pulled two tens from his wallet and laid them by her on the bar. "Bourbon it is. Drink it any way you want, lady." He turned away from her astonished look and faced the bartender. "This is her money, Mac. Don't let anyone fool with it. I get around here once in a while."

The man nodded. "You're Braden? Billy Cash's friend?"

"Right."

"No one will bother her money."

"Okay. When Billy comes in, tell him I want to see him. I'll be back." He quit the bar, walked to his car and drove off.

At nine o'clock the same morning he drove onto Armstrong's lot. He'd returned to his hotel, showered and shaved, and eaten breakfast. After breakfast he called the football player and told him he'd be by to see him. Herndon was waiting.

"How's Carol?" he asked, almost before Braden stopped the car. He climbed in and rode to the back of the lot.

"You want to hear the whole story?" Braden asked.

The blond man nodded silently, cracked the knuckles of his big hands.

Braden turned on the seat to face him. "This is between you and me, Herndon. Anyone else finds out and we're all in trouble. After you hear me out, you can decide whether or not you want to do anything about it."

"Go ahead." Herndon settled back in the seat.

Braden told him about the week in the cabin and didn't leave out a word. He told him about Samson and Gretchen Koori. When he described the scene at the house in Atwater, the athlete stirred, hunching his shoulders. Finally, Braden told him about the two kilos of heroin. When he finished, he leaned back.

"Where can I find the bastards who hurt Carol?" Herndon said.

"I worked on 'em," Braden replied. "They won't be around any more."

"What about the whore?"

"Same thing."

Herndon nodded, then looked at the man in the car with him. "I don't like you very much, Braden. If you hadn't taken the narcotics, they wouldn't have hurt Carol. If you had called on the police, she wouldn't be—"

"The film, Herndon. Don't forget the film. I could call no cops—even if I'd thought of it."

"Oh." The man looked at Braden. "What's your problem, then? You give 'em back their dope and get the film. Old man Ashe pays you off and you're in business."

Braden shook his head. "No."

"No?"

"I don't want to give 'em back anything," he said, looking up at Herndon. "Don't ask me why," he said irritably. "I want the film without giving up the heroin, that's all, and I've got to figure a way to keep from getting killed." Braden sat up straighter. "I just may have an idea, but I'll need help."

Herndon looked at him skeptically. "I don't trust you, Braden."

"You'd better trust me," Braden retorted. "You don't and a lot of guys are going to see more of Carol Ashe than her family doctor gets to see."

Herndon was silent for a moment, then looked at Braden levelly. "What have you in mind?"

Braden leaned on the back of the front seat. "How many football players do you figure are in town?"

"On my club?"

"Yes."

"Quite a few, I guess. Carson has a studio job, Willie Peralta has a bar out in Boyle Heights, and Wilson . . . there's several of the guys around. Why?"

"Would they do you a favor? It's a real big one."

"Sure, I guess so. If it was important enough." Herndon frowned. "Look, Braden, I'm not getting any of my friends involved with dope. Or in trouble. Most of those guys have families, and I wouldn't ask them to stick their necks out for—"

"No trouble and no necks," Braden assured him quickly. "And nothing illegal. But it can get Carol off the hook."

"All right. Assuming I can get some of the guys, what's the next step?"

"Do you stand in good with any of the sports writers?"

"Fred Brown." Herndon didn't hesitate.

"He's a good one. Now, here's the deal."

The two men spent another fifteen minutes in close conversation. Halfway through, the big athlete's mouth curved upward in a reluctant grin. When Braden had finished, Herndon nodded his head slowly.

"It might just work, Braden." The football player started to smile. "It looks to me like the little blond girl got to you."

Braden didn't answer.

"What did she do? Make you uncover a conscience?"

Braden shrugged, then asked: "You going to help, or not?"

"I'll do what I can," Herndon said shortly. "Call me later today."

Braden nodded and left the lot.

At eleven o'clock the same morning Braden pulled into Redondo Beach. The small beach city, southwest of Los Angeles, lay under crystal-clear skies and a hot sun. He parked close to the ocean, then walked out on the pier that jutted into the lower end of Santa Monica Bay. A little over a mile out in the blue Pacific he could see the two large fishing barges, riding lazily at anchor: the remains of two coastal ships. The hulls had been stripped of masts and superstructures, making two solid barges for the use of fishermen. Braden continued down the pier.

Halfway out, he saw an open fish stall and walked up to the figure behind the small counter—a jersey-shirted man, with a dirty yachting cap resting on his head. He stood in the center of the open-fronted store, hands on hips.

"Fish, mister? Just off the boats. We got halibut, smelt, sword . . . some crabs in the tank, and—"

"No fish. You can give me some. information, though."

"Like?"

"Like where do the barge boats land?"

The man jerked his thumb over a shoulder. "Right down there."

Braden walked down the side of the narrow shack to see where right down there was located. Several float landings were visible, with stairs descending to them from a platform built on the edge of the pier. He went back to the man.

"The boats still run at night?"

"All night long."

"How many of them?"

"Two. They leave here every hour on the hour."

"Which barge do they go to first?"

"The closest one." The man leaned on the counter. "They drop off the guys who want to use the first barge, then they pick up any passengers that are ready to come in or who want to try their luck at the barge farther out. They go to the second barge, do the same thing and come on in."

Braden nodded. "You're positive they'll be running tonight, huh?"

"Sure. As long as they're catching anything out there, the boats will haul the fishermen to the barges."

"Fish running now, huh?"

"Bass. The run figures to last a few more days."

Braden thanked the man and returned to his car. He drove to downtown Los Angeles, parked in a System lot near Main Street, then walked down that tarnished thoroughfare until he found what he was looking for. A pawnshop.

He purchased a used deep-sea rod and reel, a metal tool box with lifting drawers, popular with barge, surf and pier fishermen, and a secondhand navy pea coat; also a knitted watch cap and a pair of nondescript trousers. He locked the things in the luggage compartment of the Ford, then walked to a better section of the downtown area and ate lunch. After lunch, he closeted himself in a telephone booth and called Herndon. The man answered personally.

"Armstrong's Sports Cars."

"Braden here. How'd you make out?"

"I got six guys. For sure."

"How about the newspaper man?"

"He'll be there."

"Okay. The midnight boat, Herndon. It should arrive at the pier shortly before that time. Have 'em there by then." Braden hesitated a moment. "Is the newspaperman bringing a staff photographer?"

"Yep."

"Does he know why?"

"No. I told him only what you wanted me to tell him."

"Good."

"You sure I can't come along, Braden?"

"Damned sure. No one knows about your connection with Carol. If it gets found out, everyone's in trouble. After it cools off, it won't matter so much. But tonight you stay the hell away."

"All right."

"What's your home address, Herndon?"

"I'm just above Riverside Drive. 864 Los Feliz."

Braden wrote it down on a piece of paper. "Thanks. Now, don't forget. Go home and wait. Don't come near the beach."

"Anything else?"

"No, I guess not," Braden said, added slowly, "Yeah, there's one thing. If your friends don't show, I'm a dead man." He replaced the receiver, reached in his pocket for more coins. He consulted a slip of paper, then dialed the Palos Verdes number. Wesley Pierce answered.

"Mr. Samson, please," Braden said.

"Yes, sir." There was no recognition in the voice. "He's in the living room, sir. I'll carry the extension to him."

Braden waited, finally heard Samson answer.

"Yes?"

"This is Braden."

"I've been expecting your call. I was getting a little anxious, Braden."

"Forget it. You can have your stuff tonight."

"Where?"

"Close to you. Redondo Beach. Now, listen to this carefully. I'll be on the second fishing barge around eleven o'clock tonight. You come there with the film. All of it."

"To the barge?" There was suspicion in Samson's voice. "Why do we have to—"

"We'll switch at the barge or we won't switch at all," Braden interrupted coldly. "I'll tell you this once. Be there. You can get a boat at the pier at eleven. Dress the part and come alone." There was a short silence at the other end, then Samson spoke.

"Very well, Braden, I'll be there." The man coughed slightly. "By the way, have you seen Gretchen?"

"Who?"

"Gretchen Koori. The girl in the bathing suit who—"

"Hell, no, I haven't seen her," Braden lied. "Don't forget, now. Eleven o'clock. With the film."

"I'll be there."

Braden hung up. You're damned right you'll be there. Alone? Maybe. But you'll be there for four pounds of heroin.

He drove north to Ocean Park and went to The Pig. He learned that Billy Cash was at the White City race track. It took him ten minutes to locate him after he'd arrived at the auto-racing track. The boy was in the pit area, bent over an engine. He straightened up, wiping his hands on a piece of waste.

"You need me, Braden?"

"You got an electric drill, Billy? Three-quarter inch?"

"Not here. Up where I live I got one. You need it?"

"Hell yes, I need it."

"Okay, okay. Let's go up there and I'll let you use it."

They drove to the boy's rooming house, entered the garage. Here Braden drilled six holes in the metal toolbox; two on each side and one in each end near the bottom. He put the box back in the trunk of the Ford, turned to Cash.

"You want to drive again?"

"When?"

"Tonight."

"Where, Braden?"

"Redondo.. I want you to pick me up there about nine o'clock. I'll drive down from El Segundo and you tail me in. Wait by the beach park above Manhattan Beach. I'll flick my lights a couple of times coming down the hill. You answer with yours."

"Why?"

"If anyone's tailing me, I want to know it. I'll park near the pier at Redondo and will be gone a couple of hours. When I get back, I want you to follow me to Pete Herndon's place."

"That's all?"

"That's all."

The dark-haired boy considered it. "How much?"

"Twenty dollars."

"Okay, Braden. I'll be there."

"You got a car?"

"I'll have one. Borrow it." The boy lit a cigarette. "What'll I do if you're tailed?"

"You'll drive like hell, pick me up, then lose 'em."

Cash nodded, took a deep drag on his cigarette. "How's the beetle?"

"What beetle?"

"The little square girl. The blonde."

"She's all right," Braden said shortly, climbed into the Ford.

"I liked her," the boy said, leaning on the window sill. He stared at Braden with expressionless eyes. "She's got you leaning, huh?"

"Nine o'clock, Billy. Don't miss." Braden pulled away from the rooming house, drove back to Hollywood and his hotel. As soon as he entered the room, he walked to the night table. He dialed the Citrus number. Carol Ashe answered.

"Oh, Stan!" she said. "I've been wondering when you'd call. Has anything hap—"

"Everything's working out," he interrupted. "How's the foot?"

"Better, but what are—"

"I'm in a hurry, Carol. Let me speak to the kid."

"Just a moment." There was a silence on the line, then Carol said quietly, "She doesn't want to talk to you, Stan."

"All right. I'll tell you, then. Have her phone the girl at Mario's office and arrange it so I can pick up an envelope there. She'll know what you mean. Have her do it now. I'll be at the office in fifteen minutes. Twenty at the most. Then have her drive you to Pete Herndon's apartment about ten o'clock tonight. You know where it is?"

"Yes, I know."

"I should be there sometime after midnight. With the film."

"What are you going to do?"

"Never mind," he said. "Just have her drive you there." He hesitated a moment. "I had to tell your halfback all of it, Carol."

"Oh?" Her voice was small.

"Yeah. It's all right. You'll find out when you see him."

"I hope it is, Stan. What should Jean do after she's taken me to Pete's?"

"Go home, I guess." He hung up, and for a long moment stared at the beige bedspread. He finally shook his head, dialed the L'Aiglon. He got Al Simon.

"Al?"

"Speaking."

"This is Braden."

"Oh yeah, Stan. Well, I haven't got much to report. I called a couple of people and they're working, so—"

"Hold it, Al," Braden interrupted. He waited for silence on the line. "Listen. I'm sorry I bothered you, but the deal is off. No location, no loan."

"But you said— What gives? You lost your mind or something?"

"Maybe," Braden said dryly. "Anyway, it's off. Sorry you went to all that trouble." He talked for a few minutes longer, then hung up and left the hotel.

It took him almost two hours to pick up the claim check, drive to San Fernando, retrieve the package and return to the hotel.

In his room he extracted the plastic-covered packages from the carton. He sat on the bed and studied them. He dropped one on the bed, then began tossing the other up and down aimlessly. After a while he lay back to relax. Quite a bed.

It held Stan Braden, his conscience, and a quarter of a million dollars.

CHAPTER **17**

THE night fog had wiped out the coastline, leaving the fishing barge in a world of its own. Not even the other barge was visible, and it lay but a quarter-mile away. The yellow lights pouring down on the center of the barge made the water, oily and murky to begin with, seem blacker under the swirling fog.

Braden picked a dark end of the stripped hull and arranged his gear. He had purchased live bait and was fishing. No one came near. He looked toward the coffee shack that was centered on the flush deck, then at the score of fishermen lining the low rail of the gently rocking barge. None of them would bother him. If you wanted to be part of the general camaraderie, it was easy. Just join in. If you didn't, you would be left alone to fish, or sit, or do whatever it was people did who frequented the lonely corners of the barge. He fished, waiting for the next boat to arrive.

Jean Webster. He was a son-of-a-bitch because he had kept her from making a fool of herself. It was probably the only time she'd ever cussed anyone out loud in her life. Girls like her used such expressions in the privacy of their bathroom. He grimaced. She could keep hold for twenty-five years, then give herself away to the wrong person— At the wrong time. He half-grinned. Salty little character, with her brown eyes and scrubbed neck. Warm, too. And in those pajamas . . .

The hoarse horn of the shuttle boat brought him away from the house in Atwater, and he turned to face the on-coming vessel. It emerged from the fog, running lights amber and dim, and slid up to the barge. The pilot didn't drop lines. He held the converted landing craft against the side of the barge by power alone, allowing it to inch forward. The five or six passengers stepped to the barge, and the boat began to fall away immediately.

Braden looked them over as they came aboard. Samson was there, wearing windbreaker and faded suntans and a black baseball cap over thinning gray hair. He carried a cased rod, a metal bait and tackle box. He glanced around the barge, his eyes finally coming to rest on Braden. He walked to him rapidly.

"There's no hurry," Braden said as the smaller man came before him. "You might as well relax. The boat won't be back for an hour."

Samson nodded.

"You bring the film?" Braden asked.

"Yes."

"Anyone with you?"

"No."

"Good. Let's see the film."

"My buyers are angry about this delay, Braden. They've already cut the pay-off price, and—"

"Your fault, Samson," Braden cut in flatly. "You don't take dirty pictures and force young girls to do a man's work. You're a slug, old man, and you make me sick. Open your box!"

Samson looked at him, lips thinning. He sat on a stanchion and opened the metal box. Braden took it, pulled a small flashlight from his pea coat and looked inside the box. Four circular flat cans, the type used to carry sixteen-millimeter film, rested in the bottom of the metal chest. He opened the cans and examined the film. Two prints and two negatives. He pulled out a strip of film, a foot beyond the leader, and pressed a couple of the frames against the flashlight lens.

"This must be a gem, Samson. Sound track and all."

The older man didn't comment.

"What did you do? Make her talk, too?"

"We told her what to say," the man answered, then asked, "Where is the stuff, Braden?"

Braden kicked metal with his foot. He handed the flashlight to Samson. The man leaned forward and opened the box. He peered in the interior carefully. At the bottom, surrounded by lead sinkers, extra line, plugs and other fishing paraphernalia, lay the two oblong objects. Harmless appearing in their plastic coverings.

"There's your two kilos, friend. Just keep the box and I'll keep yours." Braden turned his shoulder to the man, lit a cigarette. He pulled the box with the film closer, closed the lid and fastened it. Then he leaned against a tall stanchion and waited for the shore boat. He spoke no more to Samson.

The boat arrived at ten minutes past midnight. It tied up this time, in order to take on passengers for the return trip to the mainland. Braden didn't move, waited for Samson to get his gear together. The older man began walking up the side of the barge, preparatory to crossing to the boat.

Braden looked toward the shuttle boat and saw six large figures standing together at the rail. Herndon's football players. They were looking at the barge, seemed to be searching for someone. Braden waved, caught their attention. He pointed. One of the figures jumped to the barge, began trotting across the flat surface. He was laughing and looking back over his left shoulder.

"Pass!" On the boat, the man who had shouted stood poised, a gallon bait can cocked at his right ear. He shouted the word again, tossed the can.

Samson stood petrified at the edge of the barge, eyes darting wildly from side to side. Then focused on the moving football giant.

The glinting can made a wobbly arc through the night sky, came to nestle in the waiting hands of its receiver. The hands lovingly pulled it close to a massive chest, and their owner automatically dropped a shoulder and cut sharply to the right. Samson, the metal box, bait can, and Willie Peralta, two-hundred-pound all-Pro end, went sailing into the black Pacific.

Braden watched the box. It landed fifteen feet from the struggling Samson, rode on the murky water for a second or two. Then sea water poured into the drilled holes, and it quickly sank from sight.

In the general confusion that followed, Braden allowed himself to be pushed to the foreground. Five huge young men stood together at the edge of the barge and watched the men in the water paddle toward its edge. They reached down, pulled a dripping Samson from the water, then big, dark Peralta. It was then the night was lit by the brilliance of flash bulbs.

"Jesus, mister, I'm sorry." Peralta was ineffectually trying to wipe off the soaked man. "Those damned fools—"

"What's your name, mister?" A suited man, notebook in hand, crowded to the front. "We got pictures of you and Willie. Early edition tomorrow morning. This should gas you, fella! Into the drink with the best offensive end in this conference. What's the name, huh?"

"No name." Samson seemed stunned.

"His name is Clarence Samson," Braden offered, saw the newspaperman write it down. Braden moved in closer. "He lives up in the Palos Verdes Estates."

"Look, mister." It was Peralta. He spoke to Samson. "You just send me a bill for any of your stuff that's ruined. Are you hurt at all? I hit you kinda—"

Samson shook his head negatively, let his eyes flick to Braden. They were murderous. He looked back toward the water.

The reporter stared curiously from Samson to Braden. He frowned, spoke to Braden. "This guy acts like he's mad at you, mister. Instead of Willie."

"He is." Braden smiled. "My name is Stanley Braden. Mr. Samson and I had quite an argument out here. Business. In fact, at one time or another, I believe he threatened to kill me." He looked at the still-dripping Samson. "I guess Mr. Peralta cooled him off some." He turned back to the sports writer. "Did I get in any of the pictures?"

"Sure." The reporter was looking at them both. "Do either of you want prints? You can call at the paper and get a set."

"I'll be down," Braden promised, turned to Samson. "How about you, Clarence?"

Samson glared at him, stumbled toward the shuttle boat.

Five minutes later Braden joined him. As the boat pulled away, he watched the barge disappear in the fog. They were in a secluded corner by the deckhouse, hidden from the other passengers.

"Football players, Samson, and a newspaper man. They were out here to get some off-season publicity shots for the sports pages. The reporter was Fred Brown. He's the sportswriter that follows the club."

"Someone's going to look you up, Braden." The man's face was livid with anger. "You can be sure of that. If it wasn't for your insistence on meeting out here, this wouldn't have happened. I'm not taking a loss like this for—"

"You're not going to do a damned thing, Samson, except keep your mouth shut," Braden snapped.

Samson's eyes batted. "No one beats me for a hundred grand," he said, shaking his head. "Whoever is responsible gets hurt and you can bet—"

Braden laughed. "Whoever? What you going to do, old man? Shoot the whole Ram football team? Have Dutch work on the entire club? Forget it. You ran into one of those Act of God deals, Samson. Like an earthquake or a flood. Or when a movie star gets pregnant." He shrugged. "What do you do about an Act of God? Argue about it?"

"If you hadn't put your nose in the deal in the first place, this wouldn't have happened," Samson said. "Maybe I'll tell my buyers what happened. They're big enough to hurt you,

Braden. They're syndicated and they won't like missing out on this buy."

"You get me hurt and you're dead," Braden said, pulled the older man around to face him. "Now I'm going to tell you something. You'd better listen."

Samson stared at him, eyes slitted.

"You're a bungler, Samson. I told you that at Palos Verdes. Now I'll tell you something else. The Koori woman tried to double-cross you. She came to my hotel, played footsie with me, and tried to get me to blow with all the stuff. With her. When that didn't come off, she had two hoods work on Carol Ashe. They were trying to find out where the stuff was located, but the girl didn't know. I walked in, in the middle of it and worked on them. After that, I took no chances on running into a gun as long as I had the heroin. That's why the meet out on the barge."

"You're lying!" Samson whispered.

Braden ignored him. "I think I have her and her two boys scared off. I fixed it so that if I'm hurt, they get picked up. If that happens, Gretchen will turn on you like a snake. You can believe that. Here's something else. That photographer out there got some good shots. Of you and the football players. And me. They keep the negatives, Samson. Anything happens to me, Brown will remember tonight. They got your name and where you live. So they'll find the dirt racket and they might find that you've been fooling with narcotics. There isn't any way you can cover me up so it can't be traced back to you."

Samson had listened, face set. "I think you may have planned this, Braden," he said, voice low.

"Yeah?" Braden looked at him calmly. "You'll never know, will you? Remember one thing. If I'm dead, you're dead. Carol Ashe is clean now, and will probably stay that way. She'd like the opportunity to bury you and would in a minute, if anything happened to me."

"How about my film? It's worth plenty in—"

Braden slapped him, knocking the man's dentures from his mouth with the blow. He watched him scramble on the boat deck for the teeth. The incident went unnoticed in the dark corner. As the enraged man was getting to his feet, Braden pulled him up by the windbreaker lapels. He put his face close to Samson's.

"Don't say a word!" he said tightly. "Snivel one more time and I'll throw you off this scow. Now, get away from me!" He shoved the man roughly, turned and leaned against the rail. He looked toward the shore until coast lights began showing through the fog.

CHAPTER **18**

HE HAD no trouble finding Herndon's apartment on Los Feliz Boulevard. It was located near the bottom of the hill that led from Riverside Drive. He pulled to the curb a block before he arrived at the address and waited for Billy Cash.

The boy arrived seconds later and allowed his car to roll to a stop. He leaned over and rolled down the window closest to Braden.

"Nothing?" Braden asked.

"You're clean. Nothing behind you all night."

"Thanks, Billy. Follow me until I park and I'll give you your money."

After parking, he paid the boy off and mounted a set of outside stairs to the football player's apartment. Herndon answered the doorbell.

"Luck?" He motioned for Braden to enter. Carol Ashe and Jean Webster were watching him as he came into the large studio living room. Jean left her chair and walked to a window, standing with her back to the others.

"I asked you. Any luck?" It was Herndon.

"Here." Braden reached under the pea coat, pulled out the flat cans of film. He tossed them on the divan, next to the Ashe girl.

"Is that all of it?" Herndon asked.

"Yes. Print and negative. I'm damned sure Samson hasn't any more copies." Braden looked at Herndon. "You got a garbage disposal unit? And a pair of sharp scissors?"

"Right." The athlete sat down next to Carol. He picked up the film and held it. "The guys made it all right, huh?"

"Like they were playing the Forty-Niners. Willie Peralta made the take-out like it was for the rent." Braden smiled. "You and Carol owe 'em, Herndon. Me, too."

Herndon nodded then asked: "Samson?"

"He thought he'd have people looking for me. Then I told him how it was." Braden shrugged, looked at Jean Webster's rigid back. "I think he sees the light."

"It must have been closer than that," Carol said. She had tears in her eyes, one hand resting on top of the cans of film. "I don't know what you did, but Samson wouldn't give up that much heroin without—"

"He won't do anything," Braden said curtly, "and you won't be bothered any more. Have Herndon take you home, Carol, and tell Clay I'll see him in a couple of days."

"I'll tell him." The girl looked at Braden and smiled. "I'll tell him some other things, too. Thank you, Stan."

"Forget it." He moved to the door. "Okay if I use the Ford until tomorrow, Herndon? I'll drop it off at the lot sometime during the day."

Herndon just waved a hand.

Braden allowed his eyes to move over the entire room, paused a second when they came to the girl by the window. He nodded at the two on the divan, then left the apartment.

He was down the steps and nearly to the street before he heard the rapid clicking of high heels. He kept walking and almost reached the car.

"Stan!"

He stopped, turned around and waited as she came running down the walk. The girl slowed to a walk as she neared, finally faced him.

"Where are you going?" Jean Webster asked quietly.

He shrugged.

"Pete told me you never did intend giving the heroin back to Samson."

"So?"

"You won't have enough money to do the things you wanted, will you?"

"Why not? I still have the money from Ashe. I never intended to sell the stuff back to Samson either."

"I know it," she said, meeting his eyes levelly. "I want to apologize for what I—"

"Don't worry about it," Braden said.

"You did a good thing tonight. There are a lot of—"

"What did I do?" he interrupted. "I got rid of two kilos of heroin. Right now there are probably a half-dozen deals being made right here in L.A. for that amount. So I slowed 'em down for a few minutes. And I shouldn't have done that. If it wasn't for that girl up there, I wouldn't have taken their stuff in the first place. I have no right to interfere with anyone else's hustle."

"You don't believe that, do you, Stan?" She asked the question quietly, arms hanging by her sides.

He didn't answer.

"Pete says you took a terrible chance tonight."

"Herndon takes things too big. Besides, he's not the quickest guy in the world. One of these days he'll think about it and realize I couldn't get too far in." His mouth twisted. "If his football players hadn't shown up, I could have still made the trade. That way, nothing would have happened." He turned to go, and a new voice broke in.

"That's a God-damned lie! He coulda got killed, Miss Webster."

Braden turned quickly and saw Billy Cash push himself indolently from the fender of a parked car. His dark clothing made him almost invisible in the street shadows and darkness. He sauntered up to the girl, his hands shoved in hip pockets.

"I figured on the way up here it must've been a pay-off switch. What this guy says cinches it." He nodded at Braden. "He had me tail him. So I did. All the way from just outside El Segundo. He parked at Redondo Beach about an hour before he got on the boat and took a walk up the beach."

"You were supposed to be in the car," Braden said.

"Yeah." The boy cocked his head, moved to the girl's side. "He dumped something in the surf, then filled a couple of small bundles with sand." He looked at Braden. "I seen it, Braden. What was it? Horse?" He didn't wait for an answer. "It must've been. That Mexico trip and that crazy meet out in the ocean. I don't know what happened out there on the barge, but I hope the people you were supposed to switch with don't find out about you dumping the heroin first. You can get killed that way."

Jean Webster reached out a hand and curled it around the back of the boy's neck. She pulled him over and kissed him. On the cheek and on the mouth.

"Drive good, Billy." She held him close a moment, then let go. "I'll be coming down to watch you."

The boy smiled, unexpectedly. "Sure, baby." He started for his car. At the door he turned, eyes blank again. He looked at Braden.

"Hey, Braden, like why don't you get with it? You a square or something?" He climbed in the car, burned a fifteen-foot strip of rubber as he left.

There was a silence in the early morning darkness following the roar of the departing car. After a while, Jean Webster spoke.

"Haven't you anything more to say to me, Mr. Braden?"

He looked at her. "Yeah. I'll try the writing one time, Jean."

"Can you leave Pete's car here?"

"Sure. Why should I?"

"You know I have a car." She stepped close to him and put her arms around his neck. She grinned up at him. "Drive us home. Kid."